CUTTING THROUGH

CUTTING THROUGH

JOAN HOHL

THORNDIKE
CHIVERS

This Large Print edition is published by Thorndike Press®, Waterville, Maine USA and by BBC Audiobooks Ltd, Bath, England.

Published in 2005 in the U.S. by arrangement with Harlequin Books S.A.

Published in 2006 in the U.K. by arrangement with Harlequin Enterprises II B.V.

U.S. Hardcover 0-7862-8194-4 (Core)
U.K. Hardcover 1-4056-3620-3 (Chivers Large Print)
U.K. Softcover 1-4056-3621-1 (Camden Large Print)

The text of this Large Print edition is unabridged.
Other aspects of the book may vary from the original edition.

Set in 16 pt. Plantin by Ramona Watson.

Printed in the United States on permanent paper.

British Library Cataloguing-in-Publication Data available

Library of Congress Cataloging-in-Publication Data

Hohl, Joan.
  Cutting through / by Joan Hohl.
    p. cm. — (Thorndike Press large print core)
  ISBN 0-7862-8194-4 (lg. print : hc : alk. paper)
  1. Middle-aged women — Fiction. 2. Female friendship
— Fiction. 3. Large type books. I. Title. II. Thorndike
Press large print core series.
PS3558.O34759C88 2005
  813'.54—dc22   2005023513

To Tara Gavin and Melissa Jeglinski.
With thanks.

CHAPTER 1

It was a beautiful spring day for the drive from Hershey to Philadelphia. At nine in the morning, with the early rush over, the traffic on the Pennsylvania Turnpike was fairly light, making driving a pleasure rather than a grind.

Drawing in a deep breath of the mild, fresh-scented spring air wafting in the open driver's side window, Julia Langston softly hummed along with the music of her teen years playing on the radio's oldies station.

Her teen years. God, it seemed like forever ago. Julia's humming gave way to a half laugh, half sigh. Hell, it *was* forever ago. At least, she reflected, after twenty-two years and two kids it felt like forever.

At times, Julia amended, heaving a deeper sigh . . . minus the laugh. There had been good years, wonderful years, and there had been not-so-good years. But the past couple of years had been the worst, fraught with fear, anxiety and uncertainty, pain and distrust.

And it was all her husband's fault . . . well, at least, most of it was his fault.

The thought brought Julia up short, shaking her out of the path of depression her mind was headed for. She had been there, done that — a lot — over the previous months. She had also done the antidepressant routine.

Enough was enough.

Wasn't that the very reason she was making this drive? Why she had smiled through the giggles and teasing remarks from her teenage daughters, both of whom thought the idea of their parents having a romantic rendezvous — at their age — was not only funny but a bit strange?

At their age?

Julia winced at the memory of her sixteen-year-old daughter's words.

"What do people you and Dad's age do during a getaway? Live on the edge by staying up late and watching TV?"

Lucky for Emily she had made the remark in a teasing tone. Even so, she had set a bad example for her fourteen-year-old sister Emma. But Emma, being Emma, giggled and went right along with her sister.

"Yeah, do you turn on a racy movie —" she nearly choked on her giggles "— like the latest Disney flick?"

"That will be quite enough from you two," Julia scolded them, her tone light to conceal a twinge of hurt feelings inflicted by their ribbing.

Yes, Julia had decided, she had had enough; she had had more than enough, not only of her daughters' teasing, but of her entire domestic situation. Which was why she was making this Tuesday morning run into Philly.

Getaway?

Hah.

A *showdown* with her husband Jonathan better described her mission. And some shopping — a lot of shopping — over the next few days while she waited for him to fly into Philly from the West coast.

Would their time together end with a new appreciation of one another? Or the never-mentioned, but always underlying possibility of a permanent separation . . . even divorce?

A showdown? Or a resolution?

Julia slid out of the car, tipped the attendant as she handed him her keys, and slowly followed the bellman carrying her luggage into the four-star hotel's lobby. Head bent, she frowned as she extracted a couple more bills from her wallet to tip the bellman; she would have to get a twenty changed somewhere, she was running out of small tipping bills. She didn't notice the woman coming toward her.

"Julie?"

The voice was instantly familiar, as was the nickname she hadn't heard for some time. A forming smile erased her frown of concentration.

"Laura!" she cried.

"Julie!" Laughing, the woman flung her arms around Julia. "I don't believe it. It is you."

Julia laughed with her. "Well, of course it's me. My God, Laura, I haven't seen you in forever." Stepping back, she swept a glance over her friend. "You look great," she glibly lied, feeling a pang, for in truth her friend looked tired, and at least twenty or thirty pounds heavier than before.

"Yeah . . . sure," Laura scoffed, her expression both knowing and rueful. "Let's face facts, dear friend. I look dreadful. Tired, fat and middle-aged . . . probably because I am all three."

"You're no such things," Julia protested.

"Maybe you do look a bit tired, and you have gained a little . . ."

"A bit? A little!" Laura interrupted, laughing. "How diplomatic you are. My dear, I feel — and look — completely wiped, and I've gained thirty-some pounds since I quit smoking almost a year ago, and I'm almost forty. If that's not beat-looking, fat and middle-aged, what is?"

"You quit smoking?" Julia gave her another hug. "Oh, Laura, I'm so glad."

"Well, I wish I could say the same." She grimaced. "I'm nervous and hungry all the time, and I still have cravings for a cigarette now and then."

"All of those symptoms will go away in time, and you'll take off the weight. Besides, your heart and lungs will be a lot healthier."

"According to my doctor, they already are," Laura admitted. "And she also assured me the weight will come off."

"There you go." Julia grinned. "Other than that, how are you? Are you back, living here in Philadelphia, or just visiting your folks?"

"No." Laura shook her head. "Yes." She laughed. "I mean, I am visiting with my folks, but we're not living here. If we had moved back to Philly, I'd have called you.

11

You know that," she said, her voice scolding.

"Yes, I know that." Julia managed to smile and sound contrite at the same time.

"Well, we're still in the wilds of Maine. But maybe, hopefully, not for much longer." Anticipation brightened her eyes and her tone. "Drew had an appointment for a job interview here in town. And I've got my fingers and everything else crossed that will cross." She grinned. "I came along to have a break, let the kids drive Drew's parents batty for a while." Her grin widened. "The not-so-little darlings are staying with them. But what are you doing here in the city?" She glanced around. "Is Jon with you?"

"Not yet," Julia answered, carefully keeping her voice light. "He's attending a conference in California, but he'll be joining me in a few days, so we can have some private time together before going home to Hershey." It was her turn to grin. "Betty and Tim — you remember, Jon's sister and brother-in-law? — are looking after the girls. I drove down early to do some shopping here in town and at The Plaza and Court at King of Prussia."

"Hmmm . . . lucky lady," Laura said. "I wish I could afford to shop in something

12

other than discount . . . hey!" she exclaimed, stumbling as a man jostled her as he strode past.

"Are you all right?" Julia asked, scowling at the rude man as she grasped Laura's arm to steady her.

"Yeah, sure. I guess we shouldn't be standing here, blocking the entrance doors." She shrugged and glanced around. "And I see your bellman waiting for you in the lobby. Look, I'm going to be in town for a few days, too. Let's get together for lunch or something."

"I'd love to," Julia said. "Are you staying here, at this hotel?"

"Are you kidding? We can't afford this place. No, we're staying with my parents. The house seems so empty now that all of us kids are out on our own. Mom and Dad are glad for the company. I was just here to visit . . ." Laura came to a halt, her eyes widening.

"What's the matter?" Julia asked in alarm, glancing around to see what had startled her friend.

"For heaven's sake." Laura smacked her forehead with the heel of her hand. "Julie . . . I came into Center City to see Krissy. She's in town, too, to film a movie. She got in late yesterday afternoon and phoned my mother last night to ask about me, and I answered the phone. She's staying right here, in this hotel. I swear I'm —"

"Krissy, here, really?" Julia interrupted, incredulous.

"Yes, really. Talk about coincidence!" Laura sighed. "Honestly, Julie, I think having four kids must have killed off most of my brain cells or something. Krissy and I made a date to have lunch together tomorrow at that new restaurant —" she flicked a hand "— right across the street. Why don't you join us then?" She smiled sweetly at another man who muttered something nasty as he brushed by them.

"I'd love to," Julia said, smiling at Laura, and trying to ignore other similar mutters from the foot traffic forced to circle around them. "What time?"

"One." She flashed a teasing grin. "And don't you dare contact Krissy in the meantime," she warned, her grin widening. "Let's surprise her."

"Okay," Julia agreed. Reacting to another low, this time profane mutter, she shot a quick look over her shoulder, wincing at the expression on the bellman's face. "But for now I'd better run. The bellman is getting impatient. See you tomorrow at one."

"Right," Laura replied, giving Julia another quick hug. "And be prepared for a long, chatty, catch-up lunch," she called over her shoulder, just as Julia dashed into the hotel waving a hand in understanding.

Less than an hour later, still distracted and pleasantly surprised by her unexpected meeting with Laura, Julia stood at the long wide window, sightlessly staring at the panoramic view of the city. She was all checked into the hotel and settled into the spacious room. Her bags were unpacked, clothing either hung in the closet or folded and stashed away in one of the dresser drawers; she hadn't brought a lot of clothes, as she planned to go on a dedicated shopping tear.

But first, suddenly, Julia had a yen to talk to her mother. And why not? She hadn't talked to her in two days. Of course, the call would cost a lot more from a hotel than on the plan she used at home . . . and like a true ditz, she had forgotten to charge her wireless before leaving home, and she had free long distance on the cell phone. Fortunately, she had brought the charger with her. Julia pursed her lips, she could wait until her cell was charged and ready, but . . .

Oh, what the hell, she thought, Jonathan can afford it. Turning away from the window, she settled into the chair next to the table holding the phone. Lifting the receiver, she placed a long distance call to Florida.

In the small condo in a retirement village outside Fort Lauderdale, Grace Fritz picked up the receiver on the second ring. "Hello." Her soft voice sounded younger than her sixty-three years. Then again Julia, and everyone else, had always thought Grace not only sounded but appeared younger than her actual age.

"Hi, Mom, it's me."

"Hi, me." Grace laughed. "I haven't talked to you in an age. How the devil are you?"

"Fair to middlin'," Julia said, using one of her father's favorite expressions. "How are you?"

"Same as I was two days ago," Grace drawled. "Bright-eyed and bushy-tailed. How are the girls?"

"Same as they were two days ago," Julia drawled back. "A pain in the . . ."

"Julia Ann," her mother inserted in warning.

Julia laughed. "I'm only kidding . . . well, I mean, they can be pains at times, but right now, that's Betty and Tim's problem, since the Em and Ems are staying with them, and I'm in Philadelphia."

"Oh, that's right, you told me you were driving into Philly today. I had forgotten . . . one of my senior moments, I guess. How was the drive down?"

"Okay, but Mom, you'd never guess who I ran into as I was about to enter the hotel."

"Okay, then I give up . . . Who was it?"

"Laura. Isn't that a hoot?" Julia laughed.

"It certainly is," Grace agreed, laughing with her. "How is Laura?"

"She seems fine but —" she sighed. "She looks beat, kinda dowdy and she's gained weight . . . because she quit smoking."

"Well, that's good. Laura quitting smoking, I mean," Grace clarified. "And every woman with four kids looks beat. Is she staying at the same hotel?"

"No, with her parents. Drew had a job interview here in town and Laura came along, to have a break from the kids, she said. You won't believe it, but Krissy's in town, too." Julia went on to explain about Krissy staying in the same hotel while filming a movie in town.

"How is Krissy doing?" Grace asked.

"I haven't a clue. I haven't seen her yet.

Laura made me promise not to contact Krissy here in the hotel, so we can surprise her tomorrow when we all have lunch."

"Sounds like fun," Grace said. "It'll be like old times for you three again."

"Yes." A soft smile touched her lips.

They talked for a few more minutes, the usual family stuff, Julia bringing her mother up to date on her granddaughters, Grace filling her in on the health and welfare of her father and brother J.R.

The phone rang mere moments after Julia hung up.

"Hi, it's Laura."

"As if I didn't know," Julia said, laughing, thinking, yes, like old times again. "What's up?"

"I just talked to my mom . . ."

"So did I," Julia cut in, laughing again.

"You talked to my mom?" Laura asked in feigned astonishment.

Oh, yes, just like old times. "No, silly, I talked to my Mom . . . in Florida."

"I know. . . ." Laura's voice sounded exactly as it had at eighteen. "How is your mother?"

"She's fine, loves it in Florida," Julia said, smiling. "So does Dad. You know, the fisherman?"

"Yes. How could I forget." Laura giggled. "Remember how patient he always was with you, Krissy and me when he took us fishing with him?"

"How could I forget?" Julia repeated, giggling right along with Laura. "How he put up with us three flighty kids, I'll never know."

"Or me." Laura sighed. "God, we had some good times together. Didn't we?"

"No." Julia's voice was soft. "We had a lot of great times together."

"Yeah," Laura agreed, sighing again. "Anyway," she went on, her voice brighter, "I talked to Mom, told her I ran into you, and she asked me to invite you and Krissy to dinner tomorrow evening, said she'd love to see the two of you again. It's been so long."

"It sure has," Julia said. "You can tell your mother I'd love to come. What time?"

Laura laughed. "She said you're to come early and stay late." Laura's tone took on a shimmer of slyness. "By the way, Mom also told me she was going to invite the rest of the clan, said they'd want to see you and Krissy, too."

"Well, that should be a riot," Julia said, laughing at the mere thought of Laura's boisterous family.

After finally saying goodbye a good ten

minutes later, Julia returned to take up her position at the large window, her eyes misty with memories.

Tomorrow would be a noisy evening, she knew, but should be a lot of fun as well. Laura's parents, Janet and Pete, had always been ready for a good laugh, as had Laura's sister, Becky, and her two brothers, Richard and Daniel.

Along with the pleasure of seeing everyone again, Julia was looking forward to the meal itself. Before hanging up, Laura said her mother had promised to cook one of the meals she knew to be a favorite of the three friends. Topping it off would be Janet's special, utterly delicious and decadent chocolate cake.

Julia loved the meal mentioned, one she never cooked because her family didn't care for it, and was looking forward to enjoying it again. But even more than the meal itself, her mouth watered at the mere thought of the chocolate cake.

Thinking of food in general made her stomach growl. Julia knew she should get moving; she had made do with a piece of toast and a quick cup of coffee for breakfast, and as it was still early, she hadn't bothered to pull into the last rest stop on the turnpike for lunch or a snack.

It was now well past lunchtime, and she was beginning to get a hollow, empty feeling. Still she stood at the window, a soft smile on her lips.

Laura and Krissy.

It had been so long since the three of them had been together. And that had been a sad reunion — Krissy's mother's funeral. That had been an ordeal not only for Krissy, but for all of them. Everyone who knew her had loved Krissy's mother, one of the nicest people you could meet.

Julia sighed.

She'd get going soon, she told herself. For the moment, she was content to remember the growing-up years spent with Laura and Krissy, her very best friends.

CHAPTER 2

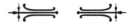

They had referred to themselves as the
Terrific Trio. Julia Fritz, now Langston,
Laura Parker, now Hartline, and Kristin
Trzcinski had been best friends since pre-
school, which in years amounted to thirty-
six, as this particular year all three women,
like it or not, would celebrate their fortieth
birthday.

It was an anniversary Julia had convinced herself was more psychological than
physical. Looking at it any other way was
too depressing.

They all grew up in Philadelphia, between Upper Darby and Drexel Hill, on
the same street in a section of neat middle-
class homes. Their parents were friends.

Of the three, Julia knew that Krissy
alone would very likely and very coolly
deny her actual age. She also continued to
maintain her maiden name . . . through
three husbands. An actress of high expec-
tations, and little apparent acting ability —

instead of taking a stage name, Krissy chose to keep her own maiden name simply because odd or different-sounding last names seemed to be in style in the business. In Krissy's opinion, Trzcinski wasn't merely odd or different, but really odd and different, not to mention difficult to pronounce, thus, she had believed, more noticeable.

Although all three were attractive, Krissy always was the real beauty of the trio. Laura was the brainy one. Julia was the levelheaded, common-sense, down-to-earth type.

The type she always considered *boring.*

Upon graduating high school, the three, then still girls in spite of being all of eighteen — and considering themselves quite mature — had sworn to be friends forever, even though they had chosen different career paths.

They had shared a wonderful summer together, and a tiny apartment in Ocean City, New Jersey, waiting tables at one of the more expensive seafood restaurants in Somers Point, a few miles right across the bay on Ninth St. from the long, narrow city billed as the family resort town.

That fall, with hugs and kisses, and more than a few tears, they separated.

Krissy went to Hollywood to pursue her goal of becoming a movie star — not necessarily an actress, but a MOVIE STAR, in capital letters. She never quite made it.

Declaring her intention to crash through the glass ceiling, become the best damned MBA, male or female, in her class, Laura went off to college in New England with a full four-year scholarship. During her sophomore year, she met Andrew Hartline, another business major whiz kid from Maine. Drew was a senior and a lover — not necessarily in that order. She immediately fell in love with him, fell into bed with him, and became pregnant by him. Laura never graduated, and she never left New England. She and Drew married and settled in his hometown in Maine. She was then all of twenty years old.

Knowing Laura so well, Julia felt certain her friend had simply decided to accept the occasion of her big four-oh. She was the type who had always simply ignored the passage of time.

Julia was the only one of the three to remain in Philadelphia and live at home. After completing a course of radiology training, she went to work as a technician in the X-ray department of a nearby hospital.

Later that same year, she met Jonathan Langston, a native of Hershey — the most good-looking, sighed-over young bachelor doctor doing his final residency at the hospital. He also was the most polite, considerate and flat-out romantic man she had ever run across.

Julia sighed at the memory she rarely revisited.

But today, with remembrances swirling in her head, the one of falling in love with Jon overwhelmed all others.

The day had been crazy, a flood of patients in the X-ray department. Julia had been on the run from the minute she had gone onto the floor at seven. It was after one before she could leave to get some lunch.

The staff lunch room was only half-full. No lineup at the cashier. Julia grabbed a packaged ham-and-cheese on a wheat roll, a ready-made salad and a large coffee. Seating herself at a table for two, she attacked her food.

"Do you mind if I join you?"

Startled by the deep, soft, bone-melting sound of the resident's voice, Julia glanced up into brown eyes the color of her favorite dark chocolate. His hair was the exact same shade. Heat ran through her, tinged her cheeks. The gorgeous Jonathan Langston wanted to join her?

"Uh . . . ummm," Julia murmured, feeling as thrilled as a teenager meeting her most adored celebrity. Telling herself to grow up, she squashed the thrill. She even managed to produce a calm reply. "No, of course I don't mind."

While Jon was in the process of unloading his tray and seating himself, Julia glanced about her. The room held even less people than when she'd entered. There were plenty of empty tables. *And he wanted to join her?*

Why?

Naturally, the first reason to jump into Julia's head was that she had somehow mishandled a plate of one of his patients he had sent up from the E.R.

Did he intend to give her hell over lunch?

Julia eyed him warily as he removed a sandwich — looked like tuna — from the plastic container, and pierced a straw through the slits on the lid of a large soda.

If she was getting a lecture, it appeared he intended to eat his lunch before delivering it. Resigned to being chastised, yet still hungry, Julia decided she may as well

26

eat her own lunch, fortify herself for the dress-down.

They had both consumed most of their food before he spoke to her again.

"Would you have dinner with me some evening, Julia?"

Julia was stunned. The best-looking guy she had ever seen wanted to have dinner with *her?* She didn't answer for a while, couldn't answer. Her heart was pounding, her throat was dry, and her mind had gone completely blank.

"Julia?" Jonathan sounded worried. "Are you searching for a polite way to turn me down?"

"No! Oh, no!" Julia blurted. "I'm just a little surprised." A little? Jeeze. She was overwhelmed. "I . . . I'd love to have dinner with you." The understatement of all understatements.

He smiled.

She melted.

"Friday is my night off this week," he said, hesitating. "Would that be too soon?"

"Friday? No, that's fine. I'm free this Friday night." This Friday? Hah, she was free most Fridays. And Saturday, and Sunday, and every other day of the week. Not that she hadn't been invited out; she had, often. And occasionally, she accepted

. . . and was always disappointed. Her mother and all her friends kept telling her she was simply too fussy.

Julia didn't care. Not for anything in the world would she admit she had this enormous crush on the new, young, totally gorgeous intern at the hospital. And now, that very same intern had asked her out for dinner.

"I get off at six," he said, thrilling her with the eager inflection in his voice. "Is seven okay?"

"Yes." Julia managed to sound almost normal. "I get off duty at four. Seven's fine for me."

"Good." Jonathan sounded and looked pleased, causing another thrill inside her.

Friday evening was more than good; it was wonderful. Before they got to dessert, Julia had progressed from enormous crush to falling head-over-heels in love with Jonathan. She prayed every night for him to fall in love with her.

Julia didn't need to pray for very long.

On their second date, Jonathan took her to dinner and a movie. Five minutes into the movie, he curled his hand around hers, lacing their fingers together. Julia's senses went bye-bye. Absorbed by the tingling sensation of his warm skin against hers, his long fingers claiming hers, she was totally unaware of where they were, the film running on the screen, the actors or the plot.

Fortunately, when they left the theater, Jonathan didn't ask her if she enjoyed the movie.

On their third date, he took her to a club with a dance floor. Before she so much as tasted her drink — a Coke, as she was still a month shy of twenty-one — he led her onto the floor, circled his arms around her waist and drew her close to him. The hard, long-muscled strength of his body pressing against hers, the warmth of his breath teasing the strands of hair at her temples, set her pulses pounding, made her own breathing shallow.

They spent most of the evening on the dance floor, his arms around her waist, her arms around his neck, lost in a world of their own, talking very little, slow dancing to even the latest, finger-snapping rock music.

On their fourth date, Julia's fate was sealed. They didn't do much of anything, as Jonathan had an early call. They didn't talk much, except to grouse about the schedule of long work hours and short amount of time off for the interns.

They had a quick meal at a chain sandwich shop in the Old City, then strolled around Independence Mall. Soon after, he drove her home and walked her to the door.

And there, on the porch, with the porch light shining on them, Jonathan drew her into a tight embrace and, lowering his head, captured her lips with his own.

His kiss was gentle, yet heated and passionate. His tongue probed delicately into her mouth. Julia felt her senses soaring, and her body melting. It was wonderful. It was heaven. It was hell when he ended the kiss and stepped back, away from her.

"I . . . er . . ." He cleared his throat, sounding as short of breath and sense as she herself felt. "I'd better go." He took a half step forward, then stepped back again. He drew a breath, a deep breath. "Good night, Julia."

"Good night, Jonathan." It was little more than a whisper, all she could manage.

He didn't look around to face her. "My family and close friends call me Jon."

"Okay." She could barely speak at all. "Good night, Jon. See you at work later?"

"Yeah." He started for the porch steps, abruptly halted, turned, and strode back to her. Pulling her into his arms, he kissed her again. Hard. When he ended the kiss this time, he didn't step back, but held on to her, raising his head to stare deeply into her eyes.

"I love you, Julia. I was gonna wait, give you time to get to know me better, but I can't." He grabbed a breath too fast for her to find words to respond. "I love you so much. I've been in love with you for months, long before I worked up the nerve to ask you out. I've seen you with the patients. You're so calm, so caring, so gentle . . . so beautiful."

Julia was stunned — thrilled, but stunned. She never thought she was beautiful. No one had ever told her she was beautiful, except her parents, and that didn't count. She didn't know whether to cry for happiness, or grab his face to pull his lips down to hers for another rock-her-world kiss. He didn't give her a chance to do either.

"Do you think . . . maybe . . ." he said with heart-melting uncertainty. "Do you think you could love me?"

"No, I don't think I could love you," she said, thrilling even more to his stricken expression. Cradling his face with her hands, she drew his mouth to within a breath of hers. "Oh, Jon, I already love you."

They were married three months later.

31

On their wedding night — because they actually waited until their wedding night — Julia learned to her delight that not only was Jon a great kisser, he was a passionate, giving lover. Jon learned — to his amazed delight — that not only was Julia a responsive and eager partner, he was her first lover.

Following what seemed like never-ending years of training and long hours with little money, Jonathan quickly became a rising young star in the field of neurosurgery, though in college-loan debt up to his eye-catching tight rear end. Julia didn't mind working to help pay off the debt . . . she was fathoms-deep in love, willing to match his long hours to make ends meet.

Although she knew she would miss being within a couple of miles of her parents, Julia also didn't mind too much relocating when Jon accepted a surprising and very flattering offer to work with a renowned neurosurgeon at the Milton S. Hershey Medical Center.

Julia laughingly told family and friends that Hershey was perfect for her, as she adored chocolate . . . and kisses.

She and Jon moved to Hershey, and shared so many kisses Julia became pregnant within six months.

Through the years, Julia, Laura and

Krissy had stayed in touch with one another, primarily by exchanging birthday and Christmas greetings, marriage and birth announcements. There were the occasional — rare actually — phone calls and get-together visits on the even more rare occasions when all three happened to be visiting family in Philly at the same time.

But, over time, even the three families drifted apart. Julia's brother, a pilot for a major airline, was based in Miami. Her parents decided to retire to Fort Lauderdale.

Krissy's mother succumbed to breast cancer. Devastated, her father sold their house and furniture and went to live with his other daughter, Krissy's married older sister, Jannette, in a suburb of Pittsburgh.

Only Laura's family stayed on in the city, parents and siblings living within several blocks of one another in the old neighborhood.

Julia's stomach grumbled, jolting her from her reverie. Grinning at the demanding noise, she turned away from the window, and the memories. Her step light, she headed for the door, intent on having lunch before indulging herself in a lavish shopping spree.

Feeling better than she had in some time, Julia strode along the hotel corridor to the bank of elevators, one thought uppermost in her mind. She hadn't fully realized how much she had missed her two best friends. It was going to be fun being with them once again.

CHAPTER 3

Pushing open the door, Julia dragged her tired body, two bulging shopping bags and a plastic dress bag, the hanger of which was hooked over and digging into her fingers, into the hotel room. Calling herself all kinds of a dimwit for not waiting for a bellman to relieve her of her packages, she dropped the bags onto the floor, draped the dress bag over the back of the settee, and crossing to the window flopped into a chair with a whooshing sigh of relief.

Forgoing her decision to have a leisurely and nutritious meal in favor of plunging, charge card first, into her shopping marathon, Julia had made do with a quick cheeseburger and soda for lunch, during which she sat all of thirty or so minutes. Other than that brief rest, she had been on the move since leaving the hotel around one-thirty.

She was more than tired; she felt thoroughly wiped out. But it had been fun.

Julia smiled. She couldn't remember the last time she had enjoyed shopping so much.

And she had spent a lot — a whole lot . . . of money. Julia's smile turned to a wince. Then she shrugged and smiled again. Because she was normally rather frugal, at least with the household money and her own personal items — if not with expenses for her daughters — Julia felt justified in having spent so much, or more accurately, charged so much. Besides, she had needed some new summer things.

Jon and the girls always teased her about wearing her clothes until they practically fell off her body — a slight exaggeration, but only slight. Her swimsuit alone was five years old, and a bit out of style. Okay, maybe more than a bit. Time for a new one, which she had bought, doing a double take at the price tag.

But the cost of the swimsuit was nothing compared to what she had paid for the dress. Never would she have believed she would pay so much for a dress — an evening gown for a special occasion perhaps, but a street-length dress?

Julia glanced at the plastic bag draped over the back of the settee, a tiny shiver of delight trickling down her spine. The garment thrilled her. It was straight, with a handkerchief hemline, black with silver serpentine lines winding their way from bodice to hem. It had two slim, adjustable shoulder straps, and came with a built-in padded-cup bra.

The very idea of actually going out without wearing a real, torturously uncomfortable strapless bra sent another shiver of delight through her.

How decadent. How delicious.

How repressed was she, anyway? Julia wryly asked herself, if the mundane idea of going without a stupid bra in this day and, yes, decadent age, could give her an exciting chill of being somehow brave and daring.

Jeeze. Her daughters, the Em and Ems, would have the snickering hysterics.

Julia dismissed these thoughts and the dress that had instigated them. She had better things to think about . . . like food.

It was now nearly seven-thirty, and the long slanting rays from the setting spring-time sun streamed through the window and beyond, bathing the surrounding tall buildings, as well as the huge statue of William Penn atop city hall, in a shower of golden light.

Hi, Billy, you look great awash in soft gold.

Laughing at her whimsical thought, Julia reached for the phone to ring for room service. It was only then she noticed the small red message light blinking.

The kids.

It was the first thought to jump into her mind . . . along with a jolt of alarm.

Jon? The alarm expanded.

Find out, idiot, Julia upbraided herself, lifting the receiver and pressing the message number. First repression, now unfounded terror. You're supposed to be the levelheaded one, remember?

"Hi." Jon's distinctive, naturally sexy low voice sent tingles dancing along Julia's spine and down the backs of her thighs, even after all this time. Amazing, she marveled, missing his next couple of words.

". . . any trouble driving into the city. I suppose you're having dinner somewhere or, knowing you, still shopping. Try not to spend all of our money. Or, better yet, try spending some of our money on yourself this time, instead of merely looking or buying for the kids." He laughed, the sound even lower, sexier than his speaking voice.

The tingle inside Julia turned into a delicious shiver . . . a feeling which, considering the distance between them — both physical and emotional — she didn't appreciate.

She had spent a good chunk of their money, she mused, without fear of angering him when he found out; Jon never did question or object to whatever amount she spent.

". . . and —" Julia had once again missed his continuing words "— I hope you've bought a special outfit or dress to wear for dinner when I get there."

Her gaze shot to the bagged dress draped over the back of the settee, then to the shopping bags she had dropped to the floor just inside the door . . . and again almost missed what he was saying.

"Have fun shopping, darling. I'll see you soon."

Darling.

Tears blurred Julia's vision, and she heaved a heartfelt, throat-tightening sigh.

After nearly twenty years of marriage, she was still fathoms in love with Jon . . . even though she was currently pissed off and hating him. She was mad and deeply hurt, because she felt certain the now very professionally and financially successful surgeon Dr. Jonathan Langston had been unfaithful to her by fooling around with his nurse practitioner, of all people.

How clichéd was that, for God's sake?

The nurse's name was Brooke. She was young, mid-to-late-twenties, damn her, with a gorgeous head of naturally blond hair. She was tall, slim, lovely, intelligent and efficient. To add insult to injury, Brooke was also very nice.

Julia had actually even liked the gorgeous would-be home-wrecker at one time.

When Julia had voiced her concern over their possible affair, Jon had denied ever having been intimate with the younger woman. He had, however, admitted to meeting with Brooke several times away from the office, and kissing her a couple of times.

Kissing wasn't intimate? Although it must have been the thousandth time she had asked herself that question, it still burned Julia's mind . . . and heart.

Julia's fear that Jon wasn't being altogether truthful with her stemmed from her common-sense nature. For one thing, she knew that women, lots of women, had been sending more-than-willing signals to her husband for years. And yet, she had never doubted his fidelity. This time was different, for several reasons.

Not the least of which was the strain that had existed between them ever since Jon had refused to perform the surgery on their daughter Emily's spine, necessitated by a disc ruptured in a fall from a horse. Jon had assisted his old mentor, Dr. Michaelson, but had remained resolute against Julia's tearful pleas to do the surgery himself.

Oh, of course, Julia was well aware how doctors, especially surgeons, were about treating family members. She even understood their position. But, when their Emily was the patient . . .

Julia had wanted only the best man for the job, and in her own and countless others' opinions, Jon was the best, and Julia couldn't get around that.

The surgery was a success, Emily's recovery complete. She was even riding again. Still, Jon's refusal to apply his considerable skill to his own child continued to cause resentment in Julia that had a damaging effect, both on their daily lives and intimate relationship.

At forty-six, Jon was a normal, healthy, passionate and sexy man, as Julia well knew. They seldom made love more than once a week, lately even less than that. But even when they did, it was not the same as before. No matter how hard she tried, and she had tried, Julia just couldn't seem to get past the residual anger and resentment inside.

Now, after so many long months of strain between them, how could she be expected to believe that he had secretly met with Brooke, kissed her, probably caressed her . . . and then walked away.

It didn't seem likely to Julia, as much as she wanted to believe it was the truth.

At present, Jon was in California, attending a medical symposium . . . supposedly without his right-hand woman — so to speak. But, who knew? Julia couldn't bring herself to phone either Jon's office or Brooke's home to be sure, afraid of what she'd learn.

Julia did love Jon. They had created two beautiful and wonderful children together. And that was why she had agreed to meet him in Philadelphia when the symposium ended — for what he called a second honeymoon, which might have been amusing under different circumstances, considering they had never had a first honeymoon.

The symposium ended Thursday afternoon, wrapping up with a banquet dinner that evening. Jon was booked on a morning flight out of LAX, due to arrive in Philadelphia around dinnertime Friday. Julia had a few more days before he joined her

— a few more days to think about where her marriage was going. Would she know by Friday where her feelings were leading her?

Julia dressed in one of her new outfits the next day.

The night before, after eating a good dinner and putting her shopping purchases away, she had talked to the Em and Ems for a few minutes, assuring the girls that, yes, she had bought each of them a small gift while on her spree. She didn't go on to reveal that the small gifts were gold charm bracelets, which both Ems had been sighing over every time they were in the mall.

Tired from the long, active day, Julia had then dropped like a stone onto the bed. She was asleep within minutes, and had slept until way past her usual wake-up time of six.

Now, standing in front of the full-length mirror mounted on one of the sliding closet doors, Julia critically studied the overall effect of the shantung pantsuit and soft silk blouse beneath.

Not bad, if she did think so herself. The celery-green color of the suit, paired with the delicate spring yellow of the featherlight, sensuous-feeling blouse, seemed to enhance the medium brown of her hair and eyes, both of which she normally considered ordinary.

"You'll do," she told herself aloud. Turning away from the mirror, her gaze collided with the clock on the bedside cabinet. The digital numbers read 12:56.

Damn, she'd have to run or be late, Julia thought, scooping up her purse as she headed for the door. Good thing the restaurant was right across the street.

She *was* late, by two minutes; she had had to wait several minutes for an elevator. And then she had to wait on line at the hostess's station.

Damn and double damn. Julia glanced at her watch. She hated being late. She felt over-warm and extremely annoyed with herself by the time she finally stepped up to the cool, calm and attractive hostess.

Julia could have happily disliked the woman, if she hadn't been so darn pleasant.

"Good afternoon." The woman flashed a friendly smile. "Sorry to keep you waiting," she apologized, actually sounding as if she meant it. "Do you have a reservation?"

"No . . . yes. I'm meeting friends. I think the reservation's under the . . ."

"Are you Mrs. Langston?"

"Yes, but how . . ." she began, only to be interrupted, if politely, for the second time.

"Mrs. Hartline was a bit early, and she gave me an excellent description of you before your other friend arrived." She smiled and gestured with a slim hand. "If you'll follow me, please."

Julia followed, her agitation soothed by the pleasantly accommodating woman. She spied her friends before they saw her approaching their table. Laura and Krissy were so busy talking, they didn't appear to notice anyone else in the room.

While still a few feet from the table, Julia halted the hostess with a touch on her arm. "I'll go on from here," she explained. "I want to surprise my one friend."

With a smile and a gracious inclination of her head, the hostess withdrew.

A laugh at the ready, Julia slowly walked to the table, waiting with eager impatience to be noticed, gazing down at Krissy's beautiful, animated face.

A moment passed, then two. Krissy was talking away a mile a minute. Julia could tell that Laura was aware of her presence by the sparkle of anticipation brightening her eyes.

Another moment passed . . . and then, as

if she were suddenly aware of being stared at, at close range, a frown of annoyance marred Krissy's smooth brow and she grew stiff. Her chin rising with regal hauteur, Krissy slowly turned her head — and immediately lost her dramatic composure.

For an instant, Krissy simply sat there, delighted surprise wiping away the frown and haughty expression. Then she damn near screeched.

"Julie." Oblivious to the startled looks sent her way from the surrounding tables, Krissy jumped out of her chair and circled the table to fling herself into the outstretched arms of her laughing friend. "I don't believe this." She shot a glance at a grinning Laura, then back to Julia. "This is incredible. It's wonderful to see you again."

"It's wonderful seeing you, too," Julia said, laughing. She gave Krissy another hug, quickly releasing her, afraid her embrace had been too enthusiastic when Krissy made a slight, quick wince. "May I join you two?"

"May you?" Krissy was laughing again. "You had better join us." She leveled a stern look at Laura. "This was a setup, wasn't it," she accused in a teasing tone, and went on without waiting for an answer.

"No wonder this third place setting wasn't removed, and you were in no hurry to order."

As soon as Julia and Krissy were seated the three friends started talking, all at the same time.

"This is so cool." Krissy.

"Yeah. I knew you'd be floored." Laura.

"I'm so happy I could cry." Julia.

"Don't you dare, because then I'll cry and my mascara will run."

"Me, too. I mean cry. I never wear mascara."

At that point, their server, a really good-looking guy in his early twenties, came to the table to take their lunch orders. They paused just long enough to quickly glance at the menu and place their orders . . . All except Krissy, who paused an extra moment to level a sidelong look of interested admiration at the young man.

He blushed and beat a hasty retreat.

The chatter immediately resumed.

"Julia, you look terrific," Krissy said, sweeping a miss-nothing glance over Julia.

"Yeah," Laura agreed, grinning. "If you didn't love her, couldn't you just hate 'er?"

"Yeah." Krissy grinned back at Laura. "And I adore that outfit."

"Well . . . thank you." Julia laughed,

flushed with pleasure. "I'm glad you love me . . . and the outfit." She returned Krissy's all-over glance. Her mass of tight-curly hair was still the same flame-shot auburn, a shade of red no artificial color or skillful hairstylists could duplicate. Her skin was still fine and smooth, flawless, nearly translucent. And Julia had ascertained, even with that quick glimpse, that her figure was damn near perfect. "Needless to say, you're as gorgeous as ever."

Krissy laughed, displaying perfect white teeth, and nearly stunned the server into dropping the glasses of white wine he was carrying to their table.

Life wasn't fair. Julia smiled inside at the thought, simply because she had had the exact same thought so many times before. Even as a child, Krissy had been a beauty. She'd always been stunning men, young and not so young, with her dazzling looks and smile.

"I work at looking good, love," Krissy blithely admitted, tormenting the fiery-cheeked server with another dazzler, just for him.

"You always have . . . or at any rate, you have since your teens," Laura said, in a dry, teasing tone.

While they ate their meals, the conversation was sporadic and general. Innocuous comments were made on the weather, the changes to Center City since last they were there. They discussed the decor, excellent service and food of the relatively new restaurant and other such scintillating topics.

It was only after they had finished eating, their plates removed and their wineglasses refilled, that they settled back and got down to some real talk.

"Laura, honey, I don't want to hurt your feelings, but you really have let yourself go."

"I know, I know." Laura sighed. "But since I quit smoking I . . ." She shrugged.

"That excuse just won't wash any more. It's been, how long now?" Krissy held up a hand to fend off an answer. "Never mind. Never mind. It doesn't matter. It's been long enough. I have an exercise DVD I can send you. As far as I'm concerned, it's as good as a personal trainer. I use it myself. I'll send along my diet program. It works." She raised perfectly arched auburn eyebrows. "Will you use them?"

"You diet and work out?" Disbelief colored Laura's voice. "Regularly?"

"As clockwork." Krissy was not about to be sidetracked. "Will you?"

"What does the diet consist of?" Laura

asked, her expression skeptical. "Rabbit food without dressing like you picked at for lunch?"

Krissy sighed. "No, it calls for real food, balanced and in moderation. I deliberately 'picked' at my lunch because I intend to pig out on your mother's dinner. So, if I send the tools, will you use them?"

"Oh, Krissy, I might give it a try, but I can't promise anything," Laura hedged. "I mean, with the kids and everything, I don't know if I . . ."

"Damn it, Laura, honey, you're going to be forty in a couple months." Krissy said, "You're a lovely woman, and it's time you got your act together and whipped yourself back into shape."

"I'm a lovely woman?" Laura choked on a disbelieving spurt of laughter.

"Well, of course you are," Krissy retorted.

"But . . ." Laura began.

"You always were," Julia inserted.

Laura shot an astounded look at Julia. "You think so, too, you always have?"

"Yes, of course I always have," she insisted, frowning in confusion.

"But . . . no." Laura shook her head, sending her dull brown hair — formerly a luxurious dark chocolate, and now badly in need of conditioning treatments, not to mention a good professional cut — flying around her shoulders. "Krissy was always the pretty one."

"No," Julia said, smiling at the redhead. "Krissy was always the beautiful one." Krissy inclined her head in acceptance, and smiled back. Julia's gaze and smile returned to Laura. "You and I had to be satisfied with being the merely attractive sidekicks."

"And quite often," Krissy said, "merely attractive matures into really lovely."

Looking flabbergasted, Laura whooshed back in her chair. "I don't believe this." Her astonished gaze shifted from one friend to the other. "You're serious. Both of you. Why didn't you ever say anything before?"

"Oh, for God's sake." Krissy slanted a bemused glance at Julia, as if seeking guidance.

"Don't look at me," Julia drawled, shrugging. "I always thought she knew what she looked like."

"Yeah," Laura inserted, "the plain Jane of the trio."

"I just might smack her for that stupid remark," Krissy informed Julia in a conversational tone, while making a point of ignoring Laura.

"Oh, please don't," Julia pleaded, the light of laughter dancing in her eyes. "At least, not here, in public."

"Oh Lord." Laura rolled her eyes. "Nothing's changed, it's just like old times. You two are nuts as ever."

"Okay, I can't slug her here." Still ignoring Laura, Krissy again spoke directly to Julia. "So, let's get out of here. We can dash right across the street, zip up the elevator to my suite, kick off our shoes and get comfortable. And then we'll beat her up."

"Sounds like a plan to me," Julia agreed, glancing around the room. "Let's get the check."

"I've already taken care of it, love," Krissy said. "I handed the waiter my credit card when he refilled our glasses." Her glance tracked Julia's. "All we have to wait for . . . ah, here he comes now for my autograph."

"But I haven't finished my wine," Laura protested, lifting the still nearly-full glass as proof.

"Oh, shut up, Laura," Krissy ordered, signing her name with a flourish on the receipt, and handing it back to the server with a mind-bending smile. He stumbled a retreat; she took a quick glance at the fabulous diamond-encrusted watch on her delicate wrist, then looked straight at Laura. "It is 2:30 now. What time is your mother expecting us for dinner?"

"She said to come anytime." She took a quick sip — gulp — of her wine. "But dinner's about six or so."

"All right." Krissy heaved a sigh as Laura took another deep swallow. "Laura, darling," she said kindly, "I have a bar in my suite. You can get sloshed there in private if you want to. May we go now?"

Julia couldn't hold it in any longer; she laughed out loud at the familiar sniping of her beloved best friends.

"You're really ticking me off, kiddo," Laura said in the most pleasant of tones, carefully setting down her now half-empty glass. "I don't want to get sloshed."

"Whatever," Krissy airily retorted, sliding back her chair and rising to her five-foot-six-inch height . . . that is in her three-inch killer spiked heels.

"I never get sloshed," Laura grumbled, trailing Julia and Krissy from the room and out the door.

"Then maybe it's time you did," Krissy shot back, leading the way across the street and into the hotel lobby. "You might as well go all the way in your obvious determination of making a complete slob of yourself."

Julia gave a soft gasp and stared at her friend; the remark was way over the line.

"Krissy." Laura's soft cry revealed deep hurt. Her eyes filled with tears.

"Oh, Laura, I'm sorry," Krissy said contritely, drawing her friend into her arms. Glancing aside, she sent an agonized, apologetic look at Julia. "Oh, God. You know how much I love the two of you." Now tears were running freely down her face. "But Laura, it breaks my heart to see you looking so tired and . . . well . . ." She paused, searching for the right, yet least hurtful word.

"Like a slob," Laura supplied, sniffling, but laughing at the same time.

"I am so very sorry," Krissy repeated, brushing her fingertips over her wet cheeks.

"I know." Laura sniffed again. "But I also know it's true. I have let myself go. Thanks, hon," she said, taking the tissue Julia handed her. She stepped back, blew her nose, then laughed. "Krissy, you should never cry, because right now, you look exactly like a raccoon."

"Oh, hell," Krissy muttered, accepting the tissue Julia offered her. "Thanks, but it's going to take more than this to repair the damage." She dabbed at her eyes, groaning when the tissue came away smeared with blackened tears. "Let's get into an elevator, for heaven's sake."

Once they were safely away from curious eyes, and inside the spacious suite, Krissy headed for the bathroom. "I'm going to clean myself up," she announced. "You guys get comfortable, help yourself at the bar." With a wave of her hand, she indicated a large credenza set against a wall, next to a plush settee.

"Wow," Laura murmured in an awed tone. "This place is something else." She opened the credenza to reveal an array of bottles. "When she said bar, I thought she meant one of those small sealed things stocked with tiny bottles of booze and snacks that cost an arm and a leg. But this . . . this is the real deal."

"Yes," Julia agreed, peering over Laura's shoulder. "It certainly is. We could have a real party."

"So what's stopping us?" Krissy walked into the room, her face clean and shiny, free of any trace of makeup, and still beautiful as ever. "We're together again." Joining her friends at the cabinet, she curled her arms around their waists. "Let's pop a cork and celebrate."

"Look, you said get comfortable," Julia said, looking at Laura. "Do you think your mother will expect us to be dressed to kill?"

"Of course not. Why?"

Julia indicated her suit and her heeled shoes. "I think I'll go to my room and change into jeans or something."

"Good idea," Krissy said. "I'll change, too."

"Hey," Laura protested. "What about me?"

"You can change when you get back to your mother's," Julia reminded her. "As you were probably planning to do anyway. Weren't you?"

"Yes," Laura admitted, her grin ruining her attempt to look sheepish.

"Uh-huh." Julia nodded and made for the door. "I'll be back in a couple of minutes."

"And so will I." Swinging around, Krissy headed for the bedroom.

"Meanwhile, what'll I do?" Laura groused.

"Make yourself useful," Krissy retorted. "Open the champagne and pour. There are flute glasses in the cabinet above the credenza."

Fifteen or so minutes later, the three of

them — two in soft faded jeans and pull-overs, the other in her "do lunch" ensemble — sat curled in chairs and the settee. They sipped champagne and caught up on the events of one another's lives since they had last been together.

While Julia readily related to her friends the good events of her life — Jon's professional and financial success; her youngest daughter's outstanding scholastic achievements; her eldest daughter's award-winning performances at local horse shows — she kept to herself the hurt and anger caused by the gnawing uncertainty of Jon's fidelity.

In turn happy and sad, Laura regaled her friends with information about her four children, the oldest just turned nineteen, the youngest not yet nine.

"I swear," she laughingly explained the last child, "I must have been out of my mind . . . or drunk."

"Drunk." Having made the pronouncement simultaneously, laughing, Julia and Krissy leaned toward each other, hooked pinkie fingers, and said, "Wish" at the same time.

After downing over half of her second glass of champagne, which had obviously loosened her tongue, Laura sadly admitted

certain knowledge of her husband's un-
faithfulness on several occasions. She then
confessed to being aware of Drew's rakish
reputation before ever becoming involved
with him, but being too infatuated with
him at the time to care.

"But now I care . . . too damn much."
She swallowed the last of her champagne,
and rapidly blinked against a rush of tears.
"I care so much I could clobber the jerk."

"Oh, Laura." Julia knew the feeling, only
too well, although she wasn't ready to join
in on true confessions. Instead, she set her
glass aside and went to hug her misty-eyed
friend.

"Men are all jerks," Krissy said with
world-weary wryness. "Every one of my
husbands cheated on me. I know, because
every one of my so-called, so-sweet Hollywood friends couldn't get to me fast
enough to tell me all about it." She
laughed, sort of. "Boy, when you have
friends like that, you sure as hell don't
need any enemies."

"Did . . . er . . . you fool around on
them?" Laura timidly asked, quickly
adding, "You don't have to answer if you'd
rather not. Just tell me to mind my own
business."

Krissy raised her brows at Julia before

aiming a dry look at Laura. "When we were growing up, did I ever lie or cheat . . . about anything?"

"No." Laura and Julia answered in unison.

"You were always straightforward and honest," Julia went on. "Even when it hurt . . . you or anybody else."

"Well, I wasn't about to change out there, either. So, no, I didn't cheat on those bastards. I also wasn't about to join in on the lifestyle of sexual fun and games and drugs of that particular Hollywood crowd."

"Any big star names we'd recognize?" Laura asked with exaggerated avid interest.

Krissy laughed. "Oh, I doubt it . . . not that I'd tell you if there were."

"So, in effect, you got the shaft for being decent." Julia's voice held bitter disgust.

Seated next to her on the settee, Krissy grasped Julia's hand. "Oh, love, don't suffer on my account." Her eyes glittered. "I was compensated . . . richly compensated. Their stupid self-indulgences gave me two valuable properties, three vehicles, and financial settlements that made me a millionaire several times over."

"Hurrah for our side," Laura cheered, punching the air in celebration for her friend.

"Is anything real out there?" Julia wondered aloud. "I always think of it as never-never land."

Krissy shrugged. "There are, of course, some people who are grounded, real. But I didn't know many of that type." She grimaced. "God, I seriously hate it out there."

"So, why don't you come back east?" Laura said, impatiently swiping the residual traces of tears from her face.

"I'm here, aren't I?" Krissy's perfectly arched eyebrows arched higher.

"To stay?" Julia couldn't believe it, and it showed in her voice. "For good?"

"I'm thinking about it. I don't know if I'll stay around here, in the Philadelphia area. I've been considering New York City. I just don't know yet, but I have put my Malibu house up for sale."

"You own a house in Malibu?" Laura looked genuinely impressed.

"Yes." Krissy nodded. "And also a horse farm in Virginia. I haven't put that on the market. I don't know yet if I will, since it's here on the east coast. What I do know is that I'm done with the whole, phony Hollywood scene."

"And jerks?" Laura teased.

"Get real." Krissy's laughter held an

60

earthy note. "I like sex . . . I would even admit to loving it."

"Who doesn't?" Laura said. "How do you think I got in this position in the first place?"

Yes, who doesn't? Julia thought, suppressing a sigh of longing for the way things used to be between her and Jon, who just happened to be a wonderful lover. "Yes, who doesn't," she repeated aloud for the benefit of her two closest friends watching her in expectation.

Obviously pleased with their response, Krissy slanted a sly smile at the other two. "At present, I'm crazily in lust with a sexy hunk named Rand Cravington . . . probably a stage name." She grinned. "But, who cares?"

"An actor?" Julia asked.

"Yes."

"A good one?" Laura probed.

"Actually, yes, a surprisingly good one. He's got the second male lead role in this movie, in which I have a very small part. That's why I agreed to do it. He'll be joining me here in a day or so." Her sly smile turned blatantly satisfied. "And he is not only handsome as sin, but positively, absolutely fantastic in bed."

"Inventive, huh?" Laura said.

"Oh, my, yes," Krissy murmured. "With the stamina of a young bull." She moved like a contented feline. "He is ten years younger than I am."

Silence for a moment. An instant really. Then.

"Here's to men," Julia toasted, concealing her true feelings of shock and envy behind a smile.

"And lovers," Krissy purred.

"The jerks."

CHAPTER 4

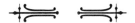

The dinner with Laura's family was a rousing success. The food, as expected, was utterly delicious. Laura's mother's specialty, death-by-suicide-chocolate cake, had been a decadent dessert. Julia, Laura and Krissy mutually agreed they had eaten too much, and didn't feel a tinge of guilt.

Everyone was in high spirits. The three friends had a head start in that department, considering the spirits imbibed in Krissy's suite. Laughter and camaraderie filled the familiar, comfortable house.

Julia became reacquainted with Drew and found him both funny and charming, and very attentive — almost loverlike — to Laura.

Although Julia exchanged a look of bafflement with Krissy she was glad for Laura; she seemed to bloom, blush like a young girl in response to Drew's attention.

His spirit appeared to be soaring, apparently in anticipation of acquiring this new job, for which he had now had two interviews.

Yet, "I'm hopeful," was all he would answer to questions from family members concerning the job, as if afraid he'd jinx his chances if he said too much.

"But, when will you know?" Laura demanded, a touch of desperation in her voice.

"I have one more interview on Friday . . . this one with the CEO of the company. I'll know then."

When Julia and Krissy said their goodbyes and headed back to the hotel, they kissed Laura farewell and promised to get together again soon.

The following two days seemed to fly by for Julia.

Jonathan hadn't called the hotel again. Not wanting to think about the disturbing possibilities why he hadn't found the time to call her back, Julia kept herself distracted by resuming her shopping whirl. Although she hadn't planned on spending any more money, she dedicated many hours to adding to the already healthy fortunes of several high-profile designers.

But the new summer clothes she purchased hadn't helped her to decide how to handle the situation with Jon. She knew she would finally have to resolve within herself the resentment she still harbored against Jon for not personally handling their daughter's surgery.

She realized her resentment was misguided. She understood Jon's reluctance. But, genuinely believing he was the best in his field in the area, she couldn't seem to get past the emotional impact of his refusal. Understanding his position, she still couldn't get around her own, even though she realized that she would have to, and soon.

As to his relationship with his nurse practitioner, whether it was still professional or had advanced into the personal, Julia finally decided there would have to be a showdown. She had to know the truth. Continuing to hide from it was taking too much of a toll on her mental state. She still loved Jon. His smile could still make her tingle. His dark gaze could still cause that melting feeling. But could she stay with him if he admitted to having been unfaithful?

Since Drew's next appointment was scheduled for Friday, Laura was hoping they could spend Thursday together.

Feeling free and unencumbered, with no kids figuratively hanging on her, she had anticipated just the two of them going off somewhere.

They had made love Wednesday night, after everybody had left and her mother's house was again quiet. It had been very satisfying, Drew proving exactly how revved he was about his prospects of getting this new job.

Even so, when Laura had suggested a day of sightseeing, Drew had shaken his head.

"I'd like to but I can't. Sorry," he said, at least sounding like he meant it. "I have some things to do before this interview tomorrow."

He didn't elaborate what those "things" were, but then, Drew rarely ever explained himself, or his actions.

Disappointed but determined not to mope around the house, squander this rare free time, Laura went out on her own to explore her old haunts.

She visited quite a few museums and art galleries, soaking up current and ancient cultures. Despite the beautiful sites surrounding her, Laura couldn't help but think of the trials and tribulations inherent in loving a man who, while claiming to love her, appeared incapable of being sexually satisfied with one woman.

For all she knew, Drew could be with another woman at that very minute. The rat. What to do? What to do? Laura repeatedly asked herself, while admiring a Rembrandt or staring down a one-eyed Picasso.

Dammit, she was not a stupid woman — except when it came to Drew. She had been pulling straight *A*s, been on the Dean's list through her sophomore year of college. Her future was looking rosy, with the possibility she might even fulfill her dream to shatter that glass ceiling.

Then she had met Drew. They hadn't been dating long before she agreed to go to bed with him. She had been a virgin; he had been very gentle with her. She fell deeply, irrevocably in love with him. By the time of final exams, she was three months pregnant.

Now almost twenty years and four kids later, Laura knew she was approaching more than her fortieth birthday; she was reaching a turning point in her life.

She cried a lot when she was alone. She felt awful. She looked a sad-sack mess. A slob, as Krissy had so correctly phrased it.

On the spot, Laura decided to accept Krissy's offer of a diet plan and workout video. She was going to pull herself back into shape, or kill herself trying. It was time, long past time to cease obsessing about Drew and take care of her own needs and desires.

That left her marriage. Should she at last boot Drew out of her life . . . or continue to play let's pretend by ignoring the problem?

One step at a time, Laura told herself, coming to a dead stop in a small, avant-garde (too avant-garde for Laura's taste) art gallery before an exhibition that appeared to be — and she feared it was — a very large dead rat affixed to an otherwise bare canvas.

Her first step was to head for the exit.

Krissy had a pleasant surprise Thursday morning. Just like a fabled princess, she was awakened by a kiss, not from some fictional Prince Charming, but from the real and exciting Rand Cravington.

Krissy had decided upon first meeting Rand that he epitomized just about every woman's idea of the handsome hero. His features were classically defined. His nose straight, narrow. His jaw firm and slightly squared. His lips were sculpted; the upper thin, the lower fuller, sensuous, denoting a passionate nature . . . which Krissy could attest to from firsthand experience.

"Good morning." His deep, smooth voice murmuring against her lips gave her shivers.

"Good morning." Krissy curled her arms around his neck, drawing him down on top of her. "Kiss me again."

His lips brushed her ear, tickling her libido. "Is that all you want, a kiss?"

"Are you serious? I haven't seen you in almost a week." Krissy laughed, soft and seductive. She raised her hands to push at his chest and slid from the bed. "While I run to the bathroom to brush my teeth, you get undressed, then into this bed, and I'll show you what I want."

Rand was happy and quick to oblige.

They spent most of the day in bed. And while resting between lusty romps with her energetic young lover, Krissy considered the other men who had paraded in and out of her life. There had been her three husbands, men she had married in good faith and with good intentions. There had been two other men she'd been involved with between her first and second marriages. They had been more friends than lovers; sympathetic listeners, willing shoulders to cry on.

Her most recent relationship was with Rand, her new, exciting lover. But the joy she might feel at this involvement was coupled with her anxiety over her ability to do justice to her part in this latest movie. The location of the filming and the fact that Rand had a major role in the movie had been her reasons for accepting the small but challenging part.

Her relationship with Rand, Krissy knew, wouldn't last . . . there was too much of an age difference. But on reflection, maybe that was for the best, because she was growing seriously fond of him. Krissy shuddered at even thinking any descriptive word stronger than fond in regards to Rand, or any man, for that matter. She had been hurt too many times before to even think about it. And now, after taking on this part, she was scared silly that she'd screw up in the movie.

There was also another small item looming large in the back of Krissy's mind, where she had fearfully shoved it. While showering, she had recently felt a lump in her left breast, tiny, but there. She felt slight twinges of pain when Rand caressed her breast a certain way.

Had it been there before, unnoticed? Krissy didn't know, didn't want to know, didn't want to think about it. Thinking about it filled her mind with abject terror.

CHAPTER 5

Friday afternoon, having managed to change his ticket and get onto the earliest flight out of LAX, and with the good fortune of a strong tailwind, Jonathan arrived in Philadelphia a few hours ahead of schedule.

He was anxious and determined to finally cement the rift between him and Julia over his stupid flirtation — and that's all it had been — with his nurse practitioner. Jon was not only disappointed but a bit disgruntled to find their hotel room empty, his wife off shopping.

With time to kill heavy on his hands, Jon showered, shaved and changed into clean, more comfortable clothes. He ordered a snack and a couple bottles of beer from room service, and sat down to wait for Julia and the opportunity to finally talk about Brooke.

He had not been intimate with his assistant. He had been tempted. After the cool, halfhearted reception he had been receiving in bed from Julia for some time now . . . hell, yes, he'd been tempted. Brooke was young, lovely and willing. So he had kissed her a couple times, caressed her, a little bit . . . but . . .

There was always a but, Jon reminded himself. And in his case, the but was always the same. He just couldn't do it. Brooke hadn't been the first woman to tempt him in the nearly twenty years he and Julia had been together. He considered himself a normal male, blessed with a healthy sex drive, and was naturally attracted to desirable women.

But Jon had a well-developed conscience. So, though he had a keen appreciation for the opposite sex, and from time to time indulged in harmless flirtations, his conscience would not allow him to betray his marriage vows.

Besides, he truly was still in love with Julia, had loved her almost from their first meeting. It was just that, over the years, he supposed they had begun being used to each other, taking each other for granted.

Then, when Emily had taken a hard fall from her horse, he had absolutely refused to perform the necessary surgery on her. How in the name of heaven had Julia exbead her forehead and the back of her neck.

She loved storms, had since she was a child. She couldn't remember ever being afraid of them, most likely because her mother never showed fear of the weather. That was one of the reasons her mother loved Florida so much; Florida was noted for its nearly daily rain showers, not to mention thunderstorms and the dreaded hurricanes. Those her mother, father and brother took seriously.

The tree leaves rustled, then began to dance as the storm drew closer, bringing wind with it. Julia took a deep breath of the rain-scented, cooler air.

"Hey, Mom, I'm home," Emily called, coming around the porch. "I knew I'd find you out here."

"Hi," Julia said, holding out her arms for a hug. "Got chased off the court, did you?" Besides being an excellent horsewoman, Emily played a mean game of tennis.

"Yeah," the girl groused, giving Julia a tight hug and a quick kiss on the cheek. "The coach said to call it a day and the storm isn't even here yet."

"But coming," Julia said, hearing another crackle of lightning almost immediately followed by a loud rumble of rolling thunder. "And fast." She raised her face to the quickening wind, drawing the cool air deep into her lungs. She grinned at her daughter's laughter.

"You really love this weather," Emily teased. "Always have, haven't you?"

"As if you didn't know." Julia laughed and stuck her hand out from under the porch roof to feel the first large, nearly cold raindrops. "I could run out in it like I did when I was your age."

"Hey, you guys!" Emma yelled over another roll of thunder, shaking like a wet dog as she came around the porch corner. Without a care, she walked up to Julia and gave her a hug.

"You're wet!" Julia protested, laughing anyway and returning the hug.

"Actually," Emily corrected, dodging her sister's attempt to hug her, too. "She's soaking."

"No kidding, Sherlock," Emma retorted, making a face at her older sister.

"So go get changed," Julia said, just as another voice called from the porch corner.

"Why are you three standing back there?" Jon said, standing at the juncture with his hands on his hips. "When you could be sitting here in the front to watch th—"

"Dad," the Ems cried in happy chorus.

Jon? Julia thought, frowning in confusion. He rarely got home in time for dinner, never mind before then.

"There's my girls," he said, holding his arms wide, as the two launched themselves at him. He caught them up in a bear hug, and immediately pulled back the arm encircling Emma. "You're soaking wet, Em."

"That's what I just said." Emily looked smug. "I wouldn't let her hug *me.*"

"All right, Emily," Julia scolded in a mild tone. "Emma, go get changed . . . then hug your father."

Jon grinned. "Listen to your mother, kid." Turning her, he administered a light tap to her rear. "Get going."

Muttering something about cruelty to children, and being unfair, Emma stomped to the door, turning inside to slant a wide grin at her family.

"And don't throw your wet clothes on the floor," Julia called after her before she could shut the door. "Toss them into the hamper."

The door slammed shut with a bang.

"Emma," Jon yelled. "Come back here and shut the door quietly."

On the verge of yelling the same thing, Julia closed her mouth.

Emily yanked the door open, had the audacity to again grin at her parents and sister, then very carefully, quietly shut it once more.

Emily laughed once more.

Julia and Jon shared a spontaneous tender smile. Suddenly breathless, Julia felt a funny, warm sensation spread throughout her entire system.

How long had it been since they had shared such a moment of accord, gentle understanding? A sense of elation combined with an edgy nervousness stirred within her.

Jon was watching her expectantly, as if waiting for — for what? Julia asked herself, growing more edgy. Unable to come up with an answer, she turned and walked to the door.

"Oh, good grief," she said in an exaggerated tone. "I stepped out for a second to watch the storm, and completely forgot dinner in the oven." She paused in the doorway, and not turning around, tacked on, "You have time for a shower before dinner, Jon."

Escape.

Julia went still a moment as she bent to open the oven door. Escape? Escape from what? she thought, turning her face away from the rush of heat as she pulled the door open. That was an odd expression to flash into her mind. Surely she didn't think she had to escape from Jon?

Did she?

Frowning in confusion at her strange reaction, Julia grabbed two oven mitts and started to reach into the oven to remove the large oval roast pan.

"Here. I'll do that," Jon said from directly behind her, eliciting a yelp of surprise from Julia.

"Sorry if I startled you," he said, bending next to her and taking the mitts from her hands. "Stand back while I slide the pan out." He reached into the oven, took hold of the pan's handles, and sniffed deeply. "Smells good. Yankee pot roast . . . I hope?" He flashed a quick grin at her.

Julia felt a melting sensation inside. Darn the man, he did have a charming smile. Drawing a slow, hopefully cooling breath, Julia returned his grin with a bit of a shaky smile.

"Yes, pot roast." Feeling as giddy as a schoolgirl, Julia moved back, around him, ostensibly to get the long-handled cooking spoon on the countertop. In truth, she felt the need to put some distance between them.

Ridiculous, she chastised herself, feeling equally foolish for her reaction to a simple grin from him . . . after nearly twenty years of marriage.

"Back up, so I can baste the meat," Julia said, amazed at the calm sounding tone she had managed. Lifting the pan's lid, she allowed the steam to billow before spooning the dark liquid over the roast and the vegetables surrounding it. Exchanging the spoon for a fork, she stuck a piece of carrot, testing the tenderness.

"Is it soup yet?" Jon murmured close to her ear, sending a wave of warmth through her.

"Not quite," she lied, as the fork had easily pierced the carrot, and wishing he'd move, put a little space between them. "You do have time for a shower."

"Okay, I can take a hint," Jon said, softly laughing to take any implied sting from his remark. "You want me the hell out of the kitchen, and out of your road."

Emily's laughter wafted to them from the dining room, where she was busy setting the table, without even being asked to do so. Wonder of wonders!

"No comments from you, young lady," Jon ordered in a mock growl, striding to the hall stairway.

"Hey!" Emily protested. "I didn't say a word."

"Well . . . don't," Jon called from halfway up the stairs, his happy-sounding laughter a long-missing and much appreciated sound.

Humming to herself, Julia lowered the oven heat to warm and slid the roast pan back inside. Suddenly, the smile faded from her lips, the silent hum died a painful death in her throat, and the sense of contentment fled at the advance of the thought that slithered like the snake of Eden into her mind, rattling her composure, leaving suspicion in its wake.

What had occurred to make him so happy? Or was it who had happened?

Julia detested the doubt spawned by the suspicion. Was she becoming paranoid, or were there reasons for her mistrust of his apparently newfound easygoing manner?

Was she at fault for the strain in their relationship, the tension in their marriage?

Julia pondered the possibility as she automatically went about finishing the meal. She removed a dish of applesauce from the fridge, lightly sprinkled cinnamon on top, and handed the plate to Emily to set on the table.

She had been wrong from the very beginning to resent Jon for refusing to operate on Emily, she conceded. But, in her own defense, it had been a traumatic time. She had been frightened near witless by Emily's fall, the need for surgery.

Opening the bread drawer, Julia took out a long, narrow loaf of French bread and slid it into the oven next to the roast pan to warm.

Her fear and anxiety had expanded into inner panic when Dr. Michaelson told her that even with the surgery, there was still a chance Emily would be paralyzed for life. It was then she had begged, pleaded almost hysterically with Jon to perform the surgery himself. And he had stood firm in his refusal.

The storm still raged outside. A loud crack of lightning, followed by a boom of thunder directly overhead startled Julia out of her introspection. She shivered against a chill unrelated to the air-conditioning.

"Mom . . ." Emily's voice from the dining room archway was hesitant. "Are you okay?"

She quickly turned the beginnings of a sigh into a laugh, albeit a shaky one. "Yes, of course." Julia manufactured a smile for her obviously concerned daughter. "That was a dandy, wasn't it?" She widened the grin; it hurt her jaw. "I nearly jumped out of my skin."

The pain in her jaw was worth the effort. Emily laughed and nodded her head.

"Hey, did you guys hear that one?" Emma said, strolling into the kitchen all clean and perky.

"Could anyone miss it?" Jon walked into the room after Emma.

Julia's stomach tightened. Calling on her thinning reserves, she brightly announced, "Dinner's ready." Turning, she pulled on the oven mitts, lowered the oven door and slid the bread from the rack. Straightening, she yanked off the mitts, and handed them to Jon. "Will you remove the pan while I slice the bread?" She didn't wait for a reply, but continued, "Emily, you can get the salad from the fridge and put it on the table. Emma, you can fill the water glasses."

They moved like a well-trained team, an orchestrated action for which Julia could not take credit. Jon had instilled the discipline into his daughters the same way he had trained his surgical team, gently, quietly, but firmly.

Julia was the only one he hadn't attempted to train. Jon knew better. Julia had her own sense of discipline. She had been taught good manners at home, and learned responsibility while in training for the radiology department.

Besides, it was her kitchen, and she hadn't hesitated to make that crystal-clear to Jon from the beginning, and the girls in turn as they grew older. Naturally, any one of them could make use of Julia's kitchen, but they had better leave it as spotless as they had found it.

The meal was delicious, as Julia had known it would be. She was a good cook, taught by an even better cook, her mother. She accepted her family's compliments with graciousness and pleasure. She had Jon to thank for her daughters' quickly voiced appreciation for every meal she prepared. He had not only had a hand in instilling good manners, he never failed to be the first to offer his praise.

When he was home for a meal.

The thought burned through Julia's mind. Jon was seldom home for a meal, at least not on time. Oh, he always called her to let her know he'd be late, and why, but that didn't change the fact he was seldom home. Yet, today, he had arrived not only on time for dinner, but early enough to shower first.

Why?

The whys were always the pin, bursting her hope balloon. Of course, he always had an explanation ready, yet . . .

Dammit! Julia hated feeling suspicious about Jon, his motives, his every action. She was so immersed in her thoughts she didn't notice Emily serving the dessert.

"Fresh strawberries with real whipped cream!" Emma crowed, jolting Julia out of her musings. "Don't even tell me you picked them out of the back garden."

"Okay, I won't," Julia said, a funny twist invading her stomach when he gave her a shared-parental smile. Her return smile was a bit tentative. "But I did," she continued, sliding her gaze away from Jon, back to Emma. "The first of the season. And I must confess to tasting one or two while I washed them. . . ." She heaved a dramatic sigh. "They're delicious, sweeter than the shipped ones we'll be getting later."

"And real whipped cream, not the fat-free topping we usually have," Jon observed, raising his dark eyebrows. "Is this a special occasion?"

"Yes," Julia said, a teasing light in her eyes as she glanced at her daughters.

Obviously reading the look in her mother's eyes, and expecting a punch line,

Emily looked droll as her sister played straight man.

"Really," Emma said. "What occasion?"

"Why," Julia answered, straight-faced, "it's the first home-grown strawberries of the season, of course."

"Oh, Mom," Emma groused, grinning.

Emily laughed out loud.

"She got you, Em," Jon teased, smiling as he stood up. "I'll bring the coffee."

It was the most relaxing, satisfying meal they had shared as a family in a long time, Julia later decided as she sipped at her steaming coffee.

The girls had gone outside after clearing away the dessert dishes. Quiet — to Julia's thinking a smothering quiet — pervaded the dining room.

"Got anything on for tonight?"

Jon's question jolted Julia. She blinked, was on the point of saying no, when her memory came to life. "Yes," she answered, repressing a sigh, wondering why he had asked. "I have a meeting with the equestrian mothers' group at seven." Glancing up from her cup, she saw a brief flash of annoyance flicker over his face. Curious about that quick expression, she had to ask, "Why?"

To her disappointment, he shrugged, as

if it wasn't important. As if, after the years of tension between them, *she* was no longer important.

"Three of the new interns who finished duty at five asked me if I wanted to sit in on their poker game tonight." His attempt at a rueful smile fell on its face. "I told them it depended on your plans." He shrugged again, unconvincingly. "So, if you're going out, I might as well join them, play a couple of hours." He raised his eyebrows. "If you don't mind?"

If she didn't mind. Like he cared, Julia thought, stretching her lips into a semblance of a smile. "No, of course I don't mind," she lied, thinking she was getting much too used to lying. But, damn, he could have called her from his office, told her he would be free for the evening. She'd have gladly skipped the meeting. It wasn't as if the meeting couldn't be held without her.

Jon frowned . . . almost as if her answer wasn't what he wanted to hear. "What about Emma?"

Ah, she should have known, she reasoned, chiding herself. It had nothing to do with his not wanting to hear her answer. It was concern about having to stay home with his daughter, as if he had ever done much child minding. Julia had to fight making a rude noise, such as snorting . . . or swearing.

"Emma's going to the meeting with Emily and me." As she always does, she added to herself. Rising, she carried her still warm, half-empty cup to the kitchen and dumped it into the sink. "You go play and relax. Enjoy yourself."

"Okay, I will." Jon's voice had a tight edge of sheer male defiance.

A strange feeling ripped through Julia, robbing her breath, chilling her to the bone. Was he truly going to play cards . . . or games of another nature?

Jealousy, Julia identified the emotion churning inside. Pure green-eyed jealousy.

Dammit! Brooke couldn't have Jonathan! He was her *husband. He belonged to* her. *He may well be dallying with the younger woman. But Brooke couldn't have him.*

Julia gritted her teeth. It had been so long now since their lovemaking had been anything other than routine, simply going through the motions.

She sighed. It used to be so wonderful between them. They had come close to the way it used to be for a while at dinner. The easy banter around the table, teasing the girls, the usual family byplay.

Julia closed her eyes against the sting of memory. Their intimate moments had run the gamut from hot and fierce, to slow and easy. Gentle. Hard. Sweet. Wild.

The very idea that Jon might be sharing those same intimate moments with *her,* laughing with her, teasing, murmuring the same enticing words he'd whispered to . . .

"Mom, are you almost ready?" Emily called from the living room. "It's nearly time to leave."

"In a few minutes," Julia called back, somehow controlling her voice against revealing the pain searing her chest, grateful for the interruption to her hurtful thoughts.

Leaving the kitchen, Julia ran up the stairs to her and Jon's bedroom, and into their bathroom. Purpose hardened inside her as she pulled off her clothes and stepped into the shower stall. Settling for a quick wash, she was toweling herself off five minutes later. Eight minutes after leaving the shower, she was dressed, had applied a light coat of makeup, fixed her hair, and squirted a dash of perfume in the direction of her neck pulse.

By the time Julia ran back down the stairs, she had talked herself into being primed and ready for a battle.

She had to make things right between her and Jon again. Julia didn't know quite how to go about resolving the issues between them. But she had to think of a way.

CHAPTER 10

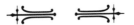

Jon sat at the table, staring at the five cards in his hand, while not really seeing them.

A tidy sum of money, change and bills, lay on the table in front of him. Another pile lay in the center of the table. He was only barely conscious of both mounds of cash. A half-empty bottle of beer sat warming at his elbow. Jon couldn't recall drinking or tasting a swallow of the brew. He hadn't touched the bowls of nuts, pretzels and chips set on a folding table near his left elbow.

His thoughts weren't centered on the game, hadn't been since the three interns and he had sat down at the table. His mind was elsewhere.

Jon had no thirst for beer or hunger for food. He was fully aware, at times painfully aware, of what he thirsted for. He needed the deep, satisfying taste of —

"What the hell, Jon?" asked Roger, the young intern at whose table the four of them had gathered. "You fall asleep with your eyes open?"

Jon blinked. "What do you mean?"

"You've been staring at your cards forever," Roger said, frowning. "Are you going to call the bet or fold your hand?"

Feeling like a complete idiot, Jon focused on his hand and cursed to himself. He was holding a full house, kings over sevens. "I'm sorry, I was a bit distracted." Damn, he thought, that excuse sounded pretty lame, even to him. "What was the last bet?"

Roger rolled his eyes as the other two men groaned. "The bet was two bucks. Josh and I have met it. Bob dropped. Are you in or out?"

"I'm in." Jon pushed two bills onto the mound. "What do you have?"

"Three jacks," replied Roger.

"Straight." Josh sighed as he folded his cards.

Jon laid his hand out. "Full house, kings over sevens. Thank you, gentlemen," he said, sliding the pile of bills onto the pile in front of him.

Josh wore a look of amazement. "I can't decide if you're flat-out unconscious . . . or just damn lucky."

Jon grinned. "Great in the O.R., too."

"So we've heard," Rob said, his expression baffled. "In fact, I've heard you're the best."

"I wouldn't go that far," Jon said, modestly, only to ruin the effect by adding, "I am pretty good, though."

All three men laughed.

Bob collected the cards and shoved them across the table at Josh. "Your deal."

Jon glanced from one to the other. "You guys sure you want to keep playing? I've taken you for a nice chunk of your hard-earned money."

"You sure have." Roger shrugged. "I guess it proves the adage, lucky in love, lucky at cards."

Jon raised his eyebrows, concealing the jolt of shock he'd felt from Roger's remark. Had he picked up something, some gossip? Surely Brooke hadn't said anything? He had been alone with her only twice. He had taken her for drinks after office hours. Two times. That was all. And he had kissed her. And yes, dammit, he had wanted to do more. But what he felt for her was only about physical attraction. And nothing else had happened.

"What's that supposed to mean?" Jon somehow managed to keep his tone even, mildly curious.

Roger laughed.

Jon cringed inside.

"You've got to be kidding, doc," Roger said, shaking his head as if in disbelief. "You gotta know you're married to one of the prettiest, nicest and most admired women around." He grinned. "And, at the risk of having to duck a punch from you, I'd go so far as to add, one of the hottest-looking."

There were murmurs of agreement from the other two men, both of whom slid back their chairs, out of Jon's reach.

Jon had to laugh at the other men's caution and the irony of Roger's statement. "So that's what the word on the street, or in this case, the word in the hospital corridors is. Julia is pretty, nice and hot."

"Looking," Roger quickly added, trying a weak and tentative smile on Jon. "And if I've insulted you —"

"You haven't," Jon assured him, his tone now easy, his smile friendly. "Actually, I'm pleased to hear others think the same way about Julia as me." His smile disappeared. His tone cooled. "Just so long as everyone remembers Julia is *my* wife. And you might pass that along."

"Yeah, sure," Roger was quick to reply. "Even though I don't think it's necessary. Julia has never been anything but pleasant to any one of us." He shrugged. "Besides, every man in the hospital respects you too much to even think about trying any fooling around."

"That's nice to know," Jon said, meaning it. "Now, you guys want to quit and leave me all this money? Or do you want to play a little while longer, try to recoup some of your cash?"

They played for another hour, an hour and a half later than the time Jon knew Julia usually returned from the Equestrian Mothers' meeting.

He was still distracted, his mind not fully on the game, but this time his lack of attention worked against him. By the time the others called it quits, he had lost at least three-quarters of the pile of bills in front of him.

Jon didn't mind. He knew how little money the interns made and was glad they had won some of it back.

While paying attention to the sparse traffic as he drove home, Jon mulled over Roger's remarks about Julia, how she was pretty, nice . . . hot.

The other men's opinion matched his own. Jon thought Julia was not merely pretty, but beautiful . . . and nice . . . and hot. She certainly could turn him on, ever since the first time he had seen her in the radiology department. His feelings for her had never changed . . . even if he had been tempted to accept what Brooke offered.

He was ashamed of his feelings, of kissing Brooke and yes, enjoying those two kisses. He was ashamed of being so damned tempted to indulge himself with a warm, receptive woman. It had been so long since he had enjoyed that sensuous intimacy with Julia.

A sigh escaped his throat. He shifted in the seat, his body made tight by a strong surge of need for his wife.

There was a time when Julia was everything to him, more important than even his career. Had she indicated an unwillingness to move from Philadelphia, he'd have chucked the fabulous opportunity to work with his idol and mentor, Dr. Michaelson. And he would have felt only slight twinges of regret for the decision.

As the old saying went, those were the days. He and Julia had laughed together, played together, even after the girls were born. They had been fantastic together in bed.

Lord, the two of them in bed. They had laughed together there, too, and played together. At times they were like kids, hiding under the covers, teasing, tickling. At other times, they were completely abandoned, luxuriating in sensuous pleasures given and received.

Compared to Julia's, Brooke's kisses were merely pleasant. Admittedly arousing, they were without the senses-rattling passion Julia could whip up in him with her hot mouth and hungry body.

The passion that hadn't been between them in a very long time.

He looked at the house to see a dim glow and sighed. A night-light. Julia had gone to bed. He glanced at his watch. It wasn't *that* late.

The flick of his remote activated the automatic door, and Jon drove into the garage. The note on the kitchen table was the first thing he noticed on entering the house. Bending over the table, Jon frowned as he read the note.

Jon, Mother called earlier. She wanted to know if we had plans for a vacation or for the 4th. When I said we didn't she asked if the girls could go down and stay with her and Dad the first two weeks in July. The girls want to go.

That was it. Julia hadn't even signed her name. He could remember when in the smallest note, Julia used to not only sign her name, but draw a tiny heart next to it.

Well, seems those days are gone forever.

Grimacing at the thought, and the realization there could be no in-depth discussions with Julia that night, Jon switched off the night-light and unerringly made his way up the stairs in the darkness.

No Fourth of July celebration. No vacation. Heaving yet another, deeper sigh, he quietly entered the bedroom, and made his way to their private bathroom, softly closing the door before turning on the light. Catching his reflection in the mirror, he made a face of distaste.

He hadn't given a thought to the Fourth or a vacation. And he should have. How long, he wondered, had it been since they had taken a family vacation in the mountains? Three, four years? Jon couldn't exactly recall, but he feared it was four. And, during those years, it had been Julia who had entertained the girls, taken them on day trips and picnics by the lake.

He had been too busy expanding his practice, honing his expertise, building his career, basking in his accomplishments. And being proud of himself, too proud, and yes, too angry to admit to Julia that he had performed the major part of Emily's surgery.

What an ass, you are, Jon told his reflection. Somewhere along the way, in your pursuit of success, you forgot you were a husband and father, as well as a surgeon.

Jon turned away from the image, tired of looking at himself, unmasked, so to speak.

He undressed and turned off the light before opening the door and felt his way to the bed. His shin made hard contact with a bedpost and he let out a muttered curse.

"Jon?" Julia asked, sleepily. She flicked on the bedside lamp.

"Yeah." Jon blinked, and focused on her as she sat up. "I'm sorry. I didn't want to wake you."

"What did you do?" she asked, smothering a yawn with her hand.

"Walked into the bedpost." Jon was quick to circle to his side of the bed while the light was still on.

"Oh." Another yawn. "Are you hurt?" she asked, a little belatedly, Jon thought.

"A bruise, no more." He shook his head as he slid beneath the covers. The bed felt cold. Jon was tempted to move closer to the warmth of her, but thought it prudent to refrain, under the current circumstances.

"Did you win or lose?" There wasn't a whole lot of interest in her tone.

"Both," he answered, a bit shortly.

"What?" She turned and frowned at him.

"I won some, then lost some, but wound up a little ahead in the end," he explained, not covering his mouth as he yawned. "The girls want to visit your folks in July?"

"You read my note?"

"Well . . . yeah." He frowned back at her.

She sighed . . . a rather long-suffering whisper of expelled breath. "If you'd prefer to discuss this in the morning . . . ?" She trailed off, dousing the light.

Jon counted to ten as she settled back under the covers. "We can discuss it now," he said adamantly, following her example, sighing as he settled in.

"Fine." She was every bit as short as he had been. "As I wrote in the note, Mother called and asked about our plans. I told her we hadn't made any, for either the Fourth or a vacation. Then she asked if the girls could visit her for two weeks . . . if they wanted to." She laughed. "Ha! As if they wouldn't jump at the chance of visiting their grandparents, and being spoiled rotten in the process, without either one of us along to interfere."

Too true, Jon thought, smiling into the darkness. "So what did you tell your mother?"

"Of course, I told her I would have to talk to you about it before making a decision."

Jon couldn't miss the hint of exasperation in her voice. "Oh, of course."

"Well?" Edgy now.

"Well what?" he retorted, quietly. "You know damn well you're going to allow them to go."

"Yes, as a matter of fact I am," she replied, her voice oh-so-pleasant. "Do you object?"

Jon was on the point of snapping "Does it matter?" but thought better of it. What was the use? It could only make things worse between them . . . if that were possible.

"No, I don't object."

"You hadn't considered something for the Fourth, or going to the mountains . . . had you?"

"No," he admitted. Truth to tell, he hadn't so much as thought of the Fourth-of-July celebration . . . never mind a vacation. He likewise admitted to himself that in all honesty, Julia had every right to be impatient with him.

145

"Well, then, it shouldn't matter," she said, the edge still clinging to her voice. "Should it?"

"No, it shouldn't," Jon said, hating the truth in the admission. "It'll probably be good for the girls to get away for a while. They haven't seen your parents since —" He broke off, simply because he didn't know how long it had been. He hated having to face that truth, as well.

"Since Mom and Dad were here for Christmas," Julia refreshed his memory in the sweetest of tones, adding, "The year before last."

Oh, sweet Christ, Jon thought, four years since they had vacationed as a family? A year and a half since Emily and Emma had seen their maternal grandparents? Was it really any wonder the distance between him and Julia had turned into a chasm? Maybe it was too late to mend the gap. Maybe, except for the girls, Julia no longer gave a rat's ass about the fraying state of their marriage.

"Have you fallen asleep?" Though very soft, Julia's voice held sharp impatience.

"No, Julia, I haven't fallen asleep," he answered, tired, but uncertain if he'd sleep at all for the rest of the night. "Was there anything else you wanted to talk about?"

"No." Julia no longer sounded sharp, weary of the discussion. "Good night."

"Good night, Julia." Closing his eyes, Jon pictured the sign on the wall above their bed. Julia had had him hang it there soon after they had moved into the big old house. The phrase on the sign was simple and profound.

Always Kiss Me Good-Night.

Jon knew there would be no kiss for him that night. Memory of former good-night kisses hurt. He had dropped the ball by refusing to tell Julia he, not Dr. Michaelson, had performed the surgery to save Emily from a life of paralysis.

No damned wonder she was little more than lukewarm when they made love. No, Langston, he snarled to himself. They hadn't made love in a long time. They had sex. The same kind of sex he could have had with Brooke.

His last thought caused Jon to go still and cold beneath the covers. The same kind of sex he could have had with Brooke *and* Julia could also have shared with another man. There were several other doctors the nurses seemed to be all moony-eyed over. And he knew firsthand that Julia was not only more than pretty and . . . hot-looking, she was loaded with sensuality.

No! The denial exploded inside Jon's head.

She wouldn't. Hadn't Roger said, and Rob and Josh agreed, that Julia was never more than friendly to everyone at the hospital?

He had to know. Even if he had to start an argument this late at night. Jon had to know. He had to . . .

Julia's soft, regular breathing filtered through the near panic seizing Jon's brain.

He couldn't wake her from a sound sleep. Despite the deep twisting pain invading his gut, Jon knew he'd be making a big mistake by waking her and demanding to know if she had been unfaithful to him.

Grimacing at the sudden reflux of his stomach, causing a sour taste of beer to sting the back of his throat, Jon slipped from the bed. Carefully he felt his way to the bathroom and the medicine cabinet where the antacids were kept.

Chewing the tablets, he decided to wait to confront Julia until the girls left for Florida. He and Julia would be alone in the house. That would be a better time.

Yes, a much better time, Jon decided, chasing the antacids with a couple sips of water before making his way back to the bed, certain he wouldn't sleep.

CHAPTER 11

A sudden sound startled Laura awake. A crackle of lightning, the rumble of thunder in the distance? Sitting up, she turned to the window, watching, listening for a repeat of the noise, the sound of rain against the pane.

Nothing.

A thousand thoughts of what could have awoken her raced through her mind. Had someone broken into the house? Was it one of the kids? Her initial alarm rapidly grew, and she reached out to shake Drew and wake him.

Beside her the bed was empty.

Dammit! Where was . . . Laura's mind stilled, caught by another sound.

She laughed with relief as she identified the noise. Their chocolate lab, Cocoa, had jumped down from the low, padded window bench. Laura leaned on her elbow to switch on the bedside lamp, blinking in the sudden brightness. Cocoa needed to go out.

Laura knew she was right when Cocoa's wet nose nudged her. The dog's large head poked over the side of the bed to touch her hand.

"Okay, okay, I'm getting up," she muttered, throwing back the cover as Cocoa started dancing in expectation of the biscuit she always received after going out.

Slipping into her mules, Laura frowned as she glanced first at the empty space beside her, then at the clock. It was after two o'clock in the morning . . . the third morning that week Drew hadn't been home in bed before 2:00 a.m.

At any other time Laura wouldn't have been aware of what time Drew got home. Busy all day, she had always been a deep sleeper. When she was out for the night, she was totally out. Never before had she heard Cocoa lightly jump from the bench to the carpeted floor. She normally wouldn't wake up until the dog had touched her with a nudging wet nose.

That was then. Since finding Megan's sickening note and key the previous week — the mere thought of the younger woman had Laura gritting her teeth — she had been sleeping in fits and starts. She hadn't said a word to Drew about the damning key — not yet ready to confront him in her startled state. She'd simply dropped the key back into the pocket of one of his other new suits.

Laura actually made a hissing sound as she pulled on her robe and followed the dog out of the bedroom door. Damn Drew, she railed. Damn his faithless soul and raging libido straight to hell and the devil.

At any other time, Laura would have felt guilty about damning her husband, but that was any *other* time. Now, fed up to her back teeth with his blatant lying and cheating, she wanted to do more than damn him. If she were a man, Laura inwardly raged, she'd beat him up and mop the floor with his worthless body.

Rather shocked by her own violent thoughts, Laura drew a deep breath to gather some measure of calm, and reached for the back doorknob. Yet just as she was about to turn the knob, it began to turn from the other side and the door was pushed in.

Cocoa dashed outside, nearly knocking Drew over as he attempted to step inside.

"What the —" he began.

Laura turned her back to him. "She had to go out." Keeping her voice level wasn't easy.

"What are you doing up at this hour?"

Was that the tone of a seriously guilty man . . . or what? Laura fumed, hardly able to believe he'd actually had the nerve to ask her that stupid question.

She'd begun to notice his uncertainty around her — his voice, his actions — ever since she had found that key. Although she'd slipped the damning evidence into the pocket of another suit, another *new* suit, he had been acting very hesitant around her.

Laura had no idea if Drew had realized the key was in a different suit, and she no longer cared. She'd stopped trying to hide her feelings. And she'd had a headache ever since.

Oh, yeah, Drew was feeling guilty as hell.

Good. Laura didn't bother to turn around. Reaching into the wall cabinet above the sink, she retrieved a bottle of aspirin and a glass. "I already said Cocoa had to go out." A low whine came from outside the door. "And now she wants to come in."

Shaking out two pills, she listened as Drew opened the door for the animal. Swallowing down the pills, she started for the hallway to the stairs, saying over her stiffened shoulder, "And now she wants her treat."

"Laura . . . ?" Drew called after her.

"Good night," she called back, silently adding, *you rotten bastard.*

Guess it was her night to shock herself, Laura thought fatalistically, mounting the stairs. Sighing for what might have been, but never was, and now never would be, she slipped beneath the covers.

Laura was still pretending to be asleep long after Drew crawled into the bed beside her, and almost immediately began to softly snore.

Maybe he wasn't feeling as guilty as she had thought. Either that, or *that woman* had worn him out.

She was now wide awake, her mind tormented by visions of Drew having sex with Megan. The mere thought of the woman and Drew writhing on a bed together brought a sour taste to Laura's throat, and a rolling, queasy sensation to her stomach.

Silently cursing, while fighting a stinging rush of tears, Laura knew she would have to do something about the situation.

There were so many factors to consider. Her tired mind rebelled at looking at each and every one. She felt trapped, her mind running in circles, getting nowhere.

The pills she had swallowed hadn't eased the pain in her head. Her temples felt as if a vise was pressing in, tighter and tighter.

She wanted a cigarette. No. She *needed* a cigarette.

Since she had quit smoking — before they had moved — she had not smoked in this house. Her new dream house. She had determined she'd never again have to listen to her kids complain about the smell of smoke in the house, in their clothes, in their hair, on Cocoa's fur, or anything else.

Since *that key day* when she had sought solace — a calming influence from smoking — Laura had gone onto the back deck every time she took a cigarette break.

But it was now going on four in the morning, and it was dark out on the deck. Her head pounded. Stifling a groan, Laura gave in to the craving.

Carefully slipping off the bed, she stepped into her slippers, grabbed up her robe, and whispered, "Come Cocoa." The dog had alertly raised her head the second she had left the bed.

Pattering at her heels, Cocoa followed Laura down the stairs. Scooping up her pack of cigarettes from the end of the countertop, she opened the door. Cocoa brushed by her to run out first, her large head lifted, her ears up, her nose sniffing the early morning air.

Smiling in spite of the drummer going berserk inside her head, Laura lit up as she stepped onto the deck. She took a deep drag and released it on a sigh.

Even at that early hour, it was warm, balmy, a sure indication of a hot day ahead. Settling into a padded porch chair, Laura smoked away. She collected her splintered thoughts, focusing her mind on the pros and cons of being separated from Drew.

There weren't any pros . . . other than the obvious one of not having to be witness to Drew's infidelity. But there was one long list of cons.

Foremost on the list were the kids. What would a divorce do to them? Laura didn't have to ponder the question. She knew the answer. While Drew was — and she suspected, always had been — an unfaithful husband, he had always been a caring, involved father.

The kids would be devastated. The very thought of telling them she and their father were separating made her head pound even more.

They had all protested against the move from Maine to New Jersey. Laura had understood their feelings. Maine was the only home they had ever known. They liked their schools. They had friends. Drew Jr. had a girlfriend and, she sighed, Jeannie had been seeing a lot of a boy in her class at school. She had cried on hearing they were moving. Now, so soon after the move, when they were still settling in, making friends, they would be devastated all over again at the mere mention of a separation and eventually a divorce.

Never mind the possibility they might have to move once more, maybe even into the city, to stay with her parents, if only for the transition period.

The pounding in Laura's head increased. Crushing the butt out in an ashtray, she immediately lit another.

Obviously satisfied the coast was clear and her mistress was safe, Cocoa came to lie down. She stretched out protectively at Laura's feet, her head resting on her paws, but her ears still on the alert.

"Good girl," Laura murmured, leaning forward to scratch behind Cocoa's ears, her favorite spot.

Cocoa whined with pleasure and Laura settled back again, avoiding the disturbing thoughts of the kids to contemplate the other cons confronting her.

There was the house. This house. The house Laura had dreamed about, longed for, ever since the day Drew slid the thin gold band around her finger.

Laura fingered the band, thinner now than before. Could she lose the house? Possibly. Very likely if Drew decided to kick up a nasty fight. Oh, he'd provide for his kids. She had no doubts on that issue. But the house had been expensive, way, way too expensive to Laura's way of thinking. But it did have four bedrooms, three full baths and a powder room. Not to mention a large family room in the basement which they had separated into two rooms, making one into a bedroom for Drew Jr., their eldest.

If they divorced, would Drew be willing to continue making the exorbitant mortgage payments, as well as child support for the three younger kids?

Laura seriously doubted it.

Then there was the fact that she had never worked, not since that summer in Ocean City when she, Krissy and Julia had been waitresses, sharing a small flat.

While Laura was willing to go to work, what could she do? Waitress again? What else was there for her? Not having finished college, she was untrained and ill-equipped to do much of anything other than housework.

The idea of doing housecleaning for someone else was out, except as a last resort. Not that Laura believed there was anything demeaning about doing housework. But she had been doing her own for what seemed forever. And she would continue to do so, if not in this house, then wherever she and the kids finally settled.

Yes. Laura gave a determined nod of her head. Housework as a profession was definitely out.

That left waitressing, or perhaps salesperson in one of the shops at a nearby mall.

Laura sighed, and lit a fresh cigarette from the old one. She'd have to be away from the house all day. As Drew Jr. would be off to college, her three youngest would be latchkey kids, on their own until she returned from work.

Laura didn't like that idea at all.

Her second oldest, Jeananne, was old enough to look out for her younger siblings, Laura supposed. Though she was not at all certain about the fifteen-year-old's sense of responsibility. At thirteen, Tim could be defiant at times — okay, most times. The youngest, eight-year-old Sue had a tendency to have a fit when things didn't go her way.

Laura herself was not the only one to blame for Sue's behavior. Being the baby, every member of the family had had a hand in spoiling her.

Still, if she did go to work, surely Jeannie, Tim and Suzzy could manage on their own for an hour or so after school.

Laura took an extra-deep drag on the cigarette, and immediately started coughing.

Damn fool! she told herself, crushing out the cigarette. She needed to go to bed, get some rest, pray the headache was gone by morning.

Hell, it was already morning. Murmuring to Cocoa, Laura pushed herself out of the chair and went back inside, the quietly obedient dog at her side. She practically had to drag her reluctant body up the stairs. She didn't want to crawl into bed next to Drew.

Tears misted her eyes. Laura shook her head, impatient with herself. No, crawling into bed with her cheating husband was the last thing she wanted to do.

What Laura really wanted to do was throw on some clothes, get into her car, and drive, drive, drive forever, somewhere, everywhere . . . anywhere Drew wasn't.

Of course, Laura wouldn't do anything of the kind. For, even though Drew was still there — if perhaps for not too much longer — so were her precious kids.

Kicking off her killer stiletto shoes, Krissy dropped into a chair. Her work was done. She had wrapped her last scene in the film less than an hour ago. Rand was still on the set, working on a love scene between him and the female lead. Krissy didn't want to watch him make love to another woman, even if it was make-believe. The actress was young . . . and beautiful.

Rand had wanted her to stay. He had even argued a bit about her decision to leave.

"This scene won't take long," he'd said, using his best coaxing tone and smile on her. "Stay. And then I can take you someplace special to celebrate."

Despite his cajoling, Krissy stood firm. "I feel beat, Rand. I'm not in a celebrating mood just now. You do your scene. I'll go back to the hotel and rest. We can go someplace for dinner this evening, if you still want to celebrate, after you see today's rushes."

"But —" he began, when the director cut him off.

"Come on, Rand, on the set," he yelled. "Let's get this scene done. Goodbye, Krissy."

Smiling, she had blown a kiss at Rand, and waved to the scowling director who, while sounding like a tyrant, was in fact a sweetheart.

Anxious to be gone, she had not bothered to remove her professional makeup. She knew that because of the mask so carefully applied by the makeup artist, she herself looked beautiful, if not as young as the other actress. She knew as well that, after she got around to cleaning her face, she would look every one of the forty years she would soon be, but refused to even think about.

Krissy really was as tired as she had told Rand. Although she hadn't had many scenes to play in the movie, tension about her performance had taken a toll. She felt weary to the bone and vaguely defeated. She had her doubts, many in fact, about her portrayal of the role. Not that she was concerned about her career. She had no intentions of ever again stepping onto a film set and in front of a camera. Still, she didn't want to be the one to ruin the movie Rand had insisted she be a part of.

Then there was the tension that had begun twisting through her lately, because Rand was acting more and more possessive with each passing day. He had begun

161

making demands, if in a gentle, cajoling tone. Just within the previous week he had insisted on putting a ring on her finger. He had even led her to a shop in jewelers' row to show her a set of rings, one with a large diamond solitaire, and matching diamond-encrusted band he said he could picture on her finger.

The picture eluded Krissy. She didn't want the commitment inherent with the acceptance of an engagement ring, never mind a wedding band worth a small fortune.

Though Krissy had several reasons for her reluctance, not the least her experience with "husbands," her main reason, of course, was the . . .

She shivered, hating to even think the word. But there it was, in big bold letters looming in her mind, twinging every time she moved the wrong way, when she showered and dressed and always when she and Rand made love.

Rand did adore her breasts.

Concealing her pang of pain every time he adored her one breast in particular, the one with the . . .

Lump, dammit! Krissy forced herself to acknowledge the . . . *thing* growing deep inside.

A sob rose in her throat. Sealing her lips against it, Krissy flung herself out of the chair to pace the luxurious suite. Tears misted her eyes. Sheer terror threatened to overtake her mind.

Increasing her gait, wringing her hands, Krissy circled and repeatedly recircled the roomy area. She had to get out. Go somewhere. Get away for a while. Away from Rand, where she could think. Alone.

No! Dear God, she couldn't be alone. She would do nothing but dwell on *it.*

Krissy was scared sick. Afraid. She had been terrifying herself lately with thoughts of self-destruction. Pills. A quick leap off the Ben Franklin Bridge. A razor to the wrist. Any method to avoid going through the horrible ordeal her mother had endured. The loss of hair had been nothing compared to the dreadful agony her mother had suffered. Near the end, she had crawled into a fetal position, into herself. She had not eaten, not wept, not spoken, to anyone, not even her husband and children.

"Stop it! Stop it! Stop it!" Krissy yelled aloud, shuddering, startling herself with the desperate sound of her own voice. "Just stop it and do something."

Run!

Where?

The ocean. The swish and undulating motion of the ocean had always had a calming effect on her. She would run there. It was close enough, little more than an hour away.

But not with Rand. With a sharp shake of her head, Krissy made a beeline to the phone. But not alone, either, or she seriously might be tempted to make it a one-way trip.

She knew exactly who she wanted to run with her. If she could arrange it. But, first things first.

Lifting the receiver, Krissy pressed the button for operator assistance. Minutes later the phone was ringing in the office of a realty agency in Ocean City, New Jersey. The agent identified himself on answering.

"This is Dan Albright. How can I help you?"

"How do you do, Mr. Albright, I'd —" she began.

"Dan, please," he interrupted.

"Dan," Krissy conceded. "My name's Kristin Trzcinski." She spelled it for him. "I'd like to rent an apartment for next week."

"Oh ma'am, I'm sorry —" he began.

"Please, call me Krissy."

"Okay, Krissy. But, I'm still sorry. I'm

afraid I have nothing for next week. It is the week of the Fourth, you know."

Actually, Krissy hadn't given a thought to the national holiday, and she was even in Philadelphia, for heaven's sake, where it had all started.

"Yes, I know," she smoothly lied. "But I assumed there would be something available in the upscale, highest end of the market."

Dan failed at concealing a sigh at the prospect of losing a large commission. "We're always booked solid for that week," he sadly explained. "Even in our highest end listings. So far as I know, every agency in town is fully booked."

"I see." Krissy didn't try to hide her disappointed sigh. "What about the following week?"

"I have several openings," he said. "But I must tell you, they are *very* high end."

"Give me the particulars."

Obviously reading from the lists, Dan proceeded to do so. "There are four in all, three with four bedrooms and three and a half baths, and one with three bedrooms and three baths, the one ensuite with the master bedroom. All four have large kitchens, attached dining rooms, spacious living rooms and full decks and, of course, private parking." He finished up with, "This last one is on the third level facing the ocean, with elevator, and is located within half a block from the boardwalk and ocean." He named a street.

Krissy recognized it. "I'll take it."

"Ahhh, ma'am," he quickly corrected himself. "I mean, Krissy, this condo rents for five thousand dollars a week. Paid in advance. Now, I realize there's little time for you to come down to inspect the place, but . . ."

"I'll put a check in the mail tomorrow."

He coughed. "Without seeing it?"

"Will you give me your word it's nice?"

"Krissy, I swear this place is downright gorgeous," he promised, his tone sincere.

"The check will be in the mail."

Moments later, Krissy disconnected. She immediately began pushing buttons again. Now to talk Julia and Laura into joining her for ladies' week away from it all.

Chapter 12

Julia felt exhausted, and a little down. The tiredness was from driving her daughters to the Harrisburg airport to send them to visit their grandparents in Florida. She was feeling down because, having just returned to her home, she was already missing the Em and Ems.

What would she do on her own for two weeks? Well, actually over two weeks, as her mother had insisted on making the flight arrangements and in doing so had added a few days on to the length of the visit.

Shoulders drooping, Julia went to the sink to make a pot of coffee. She rarely drank coffee at midday, but she really needed a caffeine boost.

She was sipping at her first cup of the hot brew when the phone rang.

The girls? Already? Julia thought, glancing at the kitchen clock while hurrying to the wall-mounted phone. No, she dismissed the idea, realizing it would be at least another half hour before she could possibly hear from them.

Jon? she asked herself as she reached for the receiver. But why would he call? He knew the girls' scheduled arrival time in Florida. Besides, he never called during the day. Unless there was an emergency. To Julia's near amazement, it was Jon, and no emergency.

"I'm going to be finished here around six," he said when she'd answered. "How does dinner out tonight at your favorite restaurant sound to you?"

She couldn't remember the last time she and Jon had been out alone together.

"Julia? Are you there?"

"Yes, I'm here. I — I'm just a bit surprised."

"Yeah, well, my last appointment of the day cancelled," he explained. "And, figuring you were probably missing the Ems already, I thought . . . maybe, you'd like to get out for a while."

"I'd love it," Julia said, smiling. "Should I call and make a reservation?"

"No," he said. "I already made one."

"Okay." Julia was quickly beginning to feel better, less glum. "What time should I be ready?"

"Since the reservation's for seven," he said, sounding pleased, "how about six-thirty?"

"Fine," Julia said, frowning as she heard Brooke's voice in the background.

"Okay. Gotta go, next patient is here, bye." He hung up before she could respond.

Brooke. The mere sound of the young woman's voice had the power to steal Julia's pleasure.

Not good, she warned herself, taking a deeper swallow of the cooling coffee. It was foolish to allow the sound of another woman's voice to upset her.

The ring of the phone cut across her thoughts. Relieved, Julia quickly grabbed up the receiver.

"Hi, Julia, it's me," Krissy said. "How are you?"

"I'm fine." Julia frowned at the unusual sound of tiredness in her friend's voice. "How are *you,* and how's the movie going?"

"Oh, I've finished shooting my scenes."

"You sound tired, Krissy. Are you feeling okay?"

Krissy sighed, then gave a weak attempt at a laugh. "I didn't know it was so evident. But, yes, I am tired. That's the reason I'm calling."

"Oh, Krissy, I'll do anything I can," Julia quickly assured her. "Do you want me to come into town?"

"No, no. Not that I wouldn't love to see you." This time Krissy managed a more normal, if brief laugh. "I called to ask if you thought you might be able to get away for a while."

"Get away? For how long?"

There was a moment's hesitation, before Krissy answered. "Er . . . a week?" She rushed on before Julia could get a word in. "I just rented a place down the shore in Ocean City for a week and I'd love to have you and Laura stay down there with me. Do you think you could swing it?"

"Wait, wait, wait," Julia said, laughing. "Krissy, you want me and Laura to stay with you? What about Rand, won't he be going, too?"

"No. Rand's still filming, will be for several weeks yet. Besides, I'd like the three of us to spend some downtime together. Like old times." She laughed. "Only this time we're old enough to drink."

"Well that's true. We have been for longer than I care to think about. I don't know what to say. When do you have the place?"

"The week after next," Krissy answered,

quickly adding, "I know it's short notice but . . . I need to . . . ahh . . . that is, I need a break. I'm tired and I'm going nuts about the job I did on the movie." She gave a strained laugh. "Or should I say, to the movie."

"Oh, c'mon, hon," Julia said. "I'll bet you did a great job."

"From your lips to the Creator's ear." Krissy sighed. "So, what do you think? Can you get away for a week?"

"You couldn't have picked a better time," Julia answered. "I put the Ems on a plane for Florida this morning. They'll be with my parents for a little over two weeks."

"Oh good," Krissy said, obviously relieved. "Will Jon have any objections?"

Who cares? Julia surprised herself with the immediacy of the thought. "I doubt it, he's been carrying a heavy schedule for some time now," she said, almost afraid to think he might be glad for the time alone. If he'd even be alone.

She mentally shook off the destructive thought, catching enough of what Krissy was saying to understand.

". . . and I haven't called Laura yet. But it would be great if the three of us could hang out at the shore together again. It's been sooo long. God, we were just kids the last time we were together like that."

"Yeah." Julia smiled softly at the rush of memories. "When are you going to call Laura?"

"As soon as we're finished talking."

"Then goodbye, Krissy," Julia laughed. "Let me know at once if Laura can go. Okay?"

"I will. Bye."

Julia was still smiling when the phone rang again only a couple of minutes later.

"Hi, again," Krissy said, sounding a lot brighter than she had earlier. "Laura would love to go with us. She's calling her parents now to ask if they'll keep the kids for the week, but she's almost sure they will. She sounded so excited about going, I never even thought to ask about Drew."

"This is really terrific, I hope the answer is yes from Laura's parents." Julia laughed. "Now I'm getting excited, just like when we made plans to go to the shore to work the summer we graduated."

"Yes, except this time, we don't have to work." Krissy laughed with her. "We can do whatever we want, lie on the beach, eat and drink, stroll the boardwalk, eat and drink, run down to Cape May, eat and drink. I wonder if The Ugly Mug Tavern is still there? We could run up to Atlantic City if we feel lucky —"

"Eat and drink," Julia cut in, nearly choking from trying to talk and laugh at the same time.

"Yeah." Krissy was having the same problem. "Oh, Julia, it will be such fun."

"If Laura can go."

"Right." Krissy was quiet a moment. "Do you think, maybe, her parents would be open to a bribe?"

Julia roared with laughter. "Are you kidding? Laura's parents?"

"Damn, I suppose you're right." Krissy giggled, sounding young and lighthearted.

"Oh, I can't wait. Come on, Laura. Call me."

"She can't call if you're on the phone," Julia pointed out. "Now, can she?"

"Boy, when you're right, you're right. Bye, Julia."

Julia smiled as she hung up. Her mood had lifted. She felt eager to go to dinner with Jon and, secretly, even more eager to go to the shore with Krissy and Laura. She mentally crossed her fingers that Laura would be able to go.

The bedroom phone rang as Julia was dressing for dinner. Hoping it was Krissy, and not Jon calling to tell her he couldn't make dinner because he had been called to an emergency, she lifted the receiver with trepidation.

"She can go," Krissy exclaimed, before Julia could even say hello. "Laura's parents are delighted, already talking about taking the kids to amusement parks and up to Camel Back in the Poconos for the water park. All except for Drew Jr., who has to work. Apparently, he got a summer job to earn money for college in the fall."

"That's wonderful," Julia said. "I mean about Laura . . . and Drew Jr., of course. I . . ."

"Julia?" Jon called up the stairs. "Are you almost ready? We should leave soon. It's twenty-five of seven."

"Oh, Krissy, I have to go. Jon's taking me out to dinner and he's ready to go. Can I get back to you tomorrow to make some plans?"

"Sure," Krissy said. "I should get off the phone, too." She laughed. "Rand's taking me out to celebrate the wrap-up of my scenes, and he's beginning to glare at me."

"I am not, Julia," Rand shouted. "But I am starving, and all this woman has been doing is talk on the phone."

"Goodbye, Krissy," Julia said.

"Bye," she returned. "I'll talk to you tomorrow, when Rand's working . . . and I'm not. Oh, don't worry about transportation. I'll take care of that from here." She laughed. "Now I really have to run. Rand's holding open the door. Bye!"

"Julia, didn't you hear . . ." Jon was grousing as he entered the room. "Oh, you're on the phone."

"Bye, hon," Julia said, holding up one finger to indicate to Jon she'd be off shortly.

Arching his brows, he mouthed the word *hon?*

Still smiling at the eagerness in her friend's voice, Julia replaced the receiver and turned to Jon.

"That was Krissy," she explained, stepping in front of the full-length mirror to give her appearance a final check.

Narrowing her eyes critically, she took a slow appraisal of herself. Her hair and makeup were perfect. As were the pale yellow sleeveless dress she'd chosen to wear and the strappy high-heeled sandals she'd slipped into.

She'd do, she thought.

"You look lovely. Is that dress new?"

Startled by the compliment, Julia swung around to stare at Jon. Although at one time Jon had been free in his compliments to her, it had been quite a while now since she'd heard one from him.

"Why, thank you," she said, both pleased and astounded. She had bought the dress during her Philly shopping spree. But she had worn it just a few weeks before at a hospital function they had attended.

Apparently, he hadn't noticed then. But of course, Brooke had also attended the function.

"Ready?"

The phone rang. "Let me just get that," Julia said, picking up the receiver. "Hello?"

"Is Jon there, Mrs. Langston?"

Brooke's soft but firm voice severed whatever pleasure Julia had been feeling. For just an instant she entertained the idea of saying Jon wasn't home. "Yes, just a moment." She held out the receiver to her husband. "It's for you. Your *nurse.*"

Jon gave her a puzzled look as he took the receiver. "Is there a problem, Brooke?"

Julia had emphasized the word *nurse* deliberately, knowing the younger woman would be annoyed, considering the remark an insult. After all, Brooke was not merely a nurse but a nurse practitioner.

Big deal. Julia tried to feel ashamed of the belittling thought, but she just couldn't.

The woman was after her husband, for Pete's sake.

Jon hung up the phone. She had been so into her unkind thoughts, Julia hadn't heard a word of his part of the exchange. "Trouble?" she asked, fully expecting him to tell her their evening was off and he had to return to the hospital.

Once more, he managed to surprise her. "Nothing that Brooke can't handle until morning," he said, taking her arm to lead her to the doorway. "Now, let's get the hell out of here before that damn phone rings again."

Julia's favorite restaurant was a short fifteen-minute drive from their home. A restored eighteenth-century inn tucked away off a black-topped back road, it nevertheless did a booming business. Reservations were always required.

Her meal, the house specialty and Julia's favorite, was delicious, as usual. Sighing with repletion, she sat back in her chair. "That was wonderful," she said, raising her wineglass in a silent toast to Jon. Bringing the glass to her lips, she drained the last swallow.

"Yes, it was." Jon returned the toast with his own glass. "More wine?" he asked, draining his glass.

Julia shook her head. "No."

"Dessert, then?"

"Oh, no." She laughed. "I'm stuffed. But I will have coffee."

"How 'bout a cappuccino chocolat?" he enticed, deliberately tempting her. "With whipped cream and grated dark chocolate on top of it?"

"That's practically the same as dessert," she protested.

"Yeah," he agreed. "But it's not any more filling than plain old coffee."

Julia caved, but only because she wanted the drink.

Jon ordered the drink for her and a latte for himself when the waiter approached the table.

Moments later he smiled as he watched her savor each careful sip of the hot, whipped-cream-laden beverage. "Good?"

"Heavenly," Julia said, licking the cream from her upper lip. "How's your latte?"

"Heavenly," he echoed, his smile sliding into a devilish grin.

Julia nearly choked on the sip she was just then swallowing.

"Okay?" Jon looked alarmed.

"Yes." She reached across the table to touch his hand reassuringly. "I'm fine."

And she was, Julia realized. She was

feeling good. It was like old times again with him. Laughing. Teasing. Showing concern for one another. She almost decided not to go to the shore with Krissy and Laura, not even tell Jon about the proposed trip with her friends.

Almost.

But she didn't. Instead, she decided being apart for a while might be more beneficial . . . to her. One relaxing dinner really didn't indicate a huge change in their relationship.

Besides, she was looking forward to a whole week just hanging loose with her dearest friends.

"Er . . . Krissy's call today . . ."

Jon gave her a questioning look. "Yeah, what about it?"

Julia took a quick breath and forged ahead. "She called to invite me to spend some time with her and Laura down the shore."

"Down the shore, where?"

"Ocean City, New Jersey. She's rented a place."

He looked pensive for a moment. "You want to go?"

Julia didn't hesitate. "Yes, I want to go."

"When?"

"Week after next."

"For how long?"

179

Julia again grabbed a quick breath. "A week."

"An entire week?" He sounded a bit disturbed.

"Yes." Julia strove to keep her own voice even, mild. "You have a problem with that?" Raising her eyebrows, and cup at the same time, she finished her drink.

Jon moved his shoulders in a near-shrug. "Well, no, but I mean . . . a whole week away?"

"Jon." She tried to appear calm while inside she was growing annoyed. "How many times have you been away from home four, five days at a time attending symposiums and medical conferences?"

"But that's different," he said in protest, actually looking shocked. "That's business."

Yeah, right, Julia thought, not too kindly. Business with Brooke along for non-business hours.

"Nevertheless," she said, holding on to her temper. "Since the Ems will still be with Mom and Dad, and I'll be rattling around the house for the most part on my own, I already told Krissy I'd go."

"Well, thanks for telling me." He sounded more than a little pissed.

Too bad.

Wiping her mouth with her napkin, Julia

placed the cloth back on the table. "Are you ready to leave?"

Jon tossed back the last of his latte, then wiped his mouth with his napkin. "Yeah, I am now."

They drove home in silence.

They entered the house in silence.

Giving a mental shrug, Julia headed for the stairs. "I'm going up. Good night." She started up the stairs, Jon right behind her.

"So am I."

Scintillating conversation, Julia thought, entering the bedroom and dropping her evening bag on the dressing table.

"I'm going to grab a quick shower," Jon said, disappearing into their bathroom.

Alert the media. Julia shook her head at herself for her inner sarcasm. At one time, she would have never dreamed she would ever harbor such negative feelings for Jon.

Of course, she reminded herself, that one time was several years ago.

Using the other upstairs bathroom, Julia cleaned her face and teeth. Back in their bedroom, the sound of the shower still running, she changed into a nightgown, hung up her clothes and slipped into bed, hoping to fall asleep before Jon emerged from the bathroom.

She was no sooner under the covers

when he crawled in next to her in the queen-size bed. She never expected him to move closer, slide his arm around her waist. But that was exactly what he did. She froze.

"Julia?" His voice was soft. His hand was warm. "Are you angry because I made a big deal about you going away?"

"No." Julia sighed. "Disappointed, I guess."

"You expected me to be happy about you going away with your friends for a week?" Jon's voice was still soft, but it had a slightly rough edge.

"No," she repeated, her breath catching as he slid his hand up to her rib cage. "But I did expect you to understand."

"Understand what?" His hand moved higher, covering her breast.

Startled by his action, and at herself because it felt so good, Julia stifled a gasp. "What are you doing?"

"You have to ask?" Now amusement laced his voice. His finger stroked the tip of her breast. "What is it you thought I'd understand?"

What? Oh, that. The shore. Intent on the sensations radiating throughout her body, Julia had lost the thread of the conversation.

"I . . . er, thought you'd understand my

wanting to go. You're away most of the day and . . ." She shivered as his hand moved down her torso to her belly. "And you work late most evenings." She drew a quick breath when his hand stroked over her hip to her thigh. "The house seems empty already and the girls only left this morning." Oh, oh, now his lips were at her ear, his teeth nipping the lobe. "I can't play tennis twelve hours a day and . . . *Jon,*" she cried when he cupped her with his palm.

"It's been a while, Julia," he murmured, moving to nearly cover her with his body. He kissed his way to her mouth, his body pressing against hers. His body was warm with arousal, his erection hot against her belly.

"I . . . I . . . know . . ." Her words were muffled by his mouth covering hers.

"I need you tonight." His voice was raw, made raggedy by passion.

Tonight. Julia shut her eyes. Tight. He needed her *tonight.* Well, then, if that was how it was, she thought, that's how it would be, as her restless body was telling her she needed him tonight, too.

Murmuring, "Yes," she parted her legs for him.

It was almost as good as it ever had been.

Almost.

If Jon's reaction to his climax was any indication, it was very good for him. He was sound asleep within minutes of collapsing onto the mattress beside her.

After dragging herself into the bathroom to rinse off under a pounding shower spray, Julia shrugged into a clean nightgown and slid back into bed.

There had been a time when, after making love, Jon would cradle her in his arms. He'd whisper his love for her, how good they were together, in bed and out.

That was then. This was now — and had been for some time. Without a word, whispered or shouted, he stretched out on the bed in satisfied relaxation and dropped deep into sleep like a heavy cruise ship anchor.

Julia turned onto her side, away from him. And tried to ignore the tears trickling down her face over her temple . . . to wet the pillow.

CHAPTER 13

Drew was not at all happy about Laura going away for a week with Krissy and Julia, even if Krissy was footing the bill for the apartment. He made his feelings perfectly clear. In fact, he had the gall to tell her she couldn't go.

Laura laughed in his face, surprising herself as well as her husband.

"Who do you think you're talking to?" she said, getting angry at his stern, stubborn expression. "You have no right to tell me what I can and can't do. I'm not a child, Drew."

"I know that," he shot back at her, every bit as angrily. "But I am your husband, and I do have some rights."

Husbandly rights, was it? The lousy cheat. Laura didn't hesitate to strike back at him. "Yes. You have the right to remain silent," she began, reciting the Miranda Rights. "You have the right . . ."

"Very funny," he shouted her down.

"What about the kids? Are you taking them with you?"

"Are you out of your mind?" she shot back. He knew damn well she wasn't taking the kids. She had told him that first thing. "I said they're going to stay with my mom and dad. All except Drew, he's staying here, closer to his job."

"So he'll be on his own?"

"Oh, give it a rest, Drew. Our son is nineteen years old," she reminded him. "He is six feet three inches tall and weighs all but two hundred pounds. He can take care of himself. In fact, he'd be insulted if we didn't agree."

"But . . ."

That's all the further she let him get. "Besides," she said, nicely. Way too nicely, to anyone paying attention. "You'll be here with him in the evenings. Won't you?"

He looked about to explode.

Laura defused him before he could sputter his anger all over her. "Think of it this way, Drew." She smiled serenely. "You and your son can bond. You can explain the facts of life to him. You know, those naughty birds and bees."

His face flushed. "We have bonded, and he knows all the facts about sex."

"That's correct," she retorted. "He

knows, because I had that discussion with him." Her voice took on a cutting edge. "I believe you were working late in the office that evening. Oh, I seem to recall it was until 2:00 a.m. or so."

Aha! Stumped him.

Drew's mouth worked, but nothing came out for a second. When he finally got it working again, all he could manage was a frustrated growl. "Then go. Do what the hell you want."

"I planned to all along."

Heading for the door, he snapped, "Who cares. I'm going out for a while."

"Who cares," she yelled an instant before the door slammed shut behind him.

Her breathing heavy, Laura stood stock-still, shocked at her temerity. Perhaps she should be feeling awful and ashamed of herself for shouting at her husband the way she had. But she didn't.

Laura felt as if a weight had been lifted from her shoulders. Her breathing slowed to a regular pattern. She was thrilled at having expressed herself in such no-nonsense terms.

Always before, she had backed down from an argument with Drew — and everybody else. She had always tried to keep the peace. She had that type of personality.

In fact, she and her two best friends had completely different personalities. Maybe that was why they got along so well.

Krissy had always been flamboyant, outgoing, and as they got into their teens, outrageous. Julia, on the other hand, was the calm, pleasant, get-along-with-everyone type. Laura had been into her studies, quiet, a little meek. Well, maybe more than a little, she conceded. She was, and continued to be, the one to always give in to the stronger voice.

In addition to her naturally quiet nature, respect for her husband had been instilled by the relationship of her parents. She had never heard them argue even mildly, never mind nearly scream at each other. But then, both of her parents were quiet and mild by nature. The apple didn't fall far from those two trees, she thought, halfway between amusement and sadness.

Always before, after appeasing Drew at the slightest hint of an argument, Laura had chided herself by paraphrasing the first line of an old song: I am woman, hear me whimper.

"Not any more." Laura said the words aloud, her voice strong with pride and determination. "Never again."

"Can't I even go down with you for the weekend?"

"No."

"Why?"

"Are you whining?"

"Yes." Though Rand's tone was petulant, his eyes gleamed with a wicked light. "You'll be away for a whole week."

Krissy gave him a wry look. "Which means, no sex for you for seven long days."

"Uh-huh."

"You look like a spoiled little boy." She laughed. "You know, you're an even better actor than I realized. I'm talking Academy Award quality."

Rand laughed with her. "It would be nice, but I wouldn't bet the farm on it." His laughing expression turned sly. "You know, the leading lady on our film has intimated she would just love to jump my bones."

"She's tired of living?"

Krissy raised her eyebrows, knowing Rand wouldn't cheat on her while she was away. Knowing that if he wanted someone else, he'd be honorable and tell her.

Grinning, he crossed the room to her and pulled her into his arms. "You'd kill for me?"

"Ahhh, no." She grinned back at him.

"Bummer." He appeared crestfallen.

"Oh, you're such a ham," she said, making a pretense of pushing him away.

"You wound me, woman. Now you must pay the price."

"Oh, good," Krissy said, sliding her hands to the back of his neck. "What kind of price?"

"Torture." He gave her a taste of his brand of torture by gliding his tongue down the curve of her neck.

She shivered in response. "Are we talking fur handcuffs and velvet whips here?"

Rand raised his head to give her an are-you-kidding look. "You're into that stuff?"

"No!" Krissy shook her head. "But I was beginning to fear you were."

"Nah, too kinky." Rand leaned forward to brush his lips over hers. "I'm an old-fashioned kind of guy."

"Then, what sort of torture did you have in mind?" She sighed as his mouth brushed hers once more.

"Torture of the sensuous kind. Like this." His tongue slid across the seam of her mouth and when she opened for him, Rand didn't greedily thrust inside, but slowly, excitingly, ran his tongue along her lip line.

Moaning deep in her throat, Krissy pressed closer to him, thrilling to the sensations created by his erection pressing against her.

His tongue proceeded to tease her by laving the inside of her lower lip.

"Rand." Her voice was growing husky with need.

"Yes, love?" His voice was sensuality itself.

"Kiss me." A pleading note now.

"Umm, not yet." His tongue stabbed at one corner of her mouth. "This is part of the torture."

Krissy grabbed onto his thick hair, trying to pull his mouth to hers.

He laughed, held firm, and stabbed at the other corner of her now pouting mouth.

"You're a devil," she said, spearing her hands through his hair, her fingers tingling to the silky feel of the wavy locks against her skin.

"And you love it. And me," he murmured, his mouth coming to hover temptingly over hers. "Don't you?"

"Yes and yes," she admitted, sighing. "Now, will you shut up and kiss me?"

He did. Over and over. Sweetly, hotly, hungrily. Before and after the act. An act no one could call torture, except for the most exquisite kind.

And exquisitely spent, Krissy lay content in Rand's arms, practically purring in response to the soothing stroke of his hand as it moved from her hip to her thigh. The sharp sting of pain she had felt when he was making love to her breasts had been soon forgotten once his body became one with hers.

"Are you sleeping?" His breath tickled her ear.

"No."

"Are you going to go to sleep?" He pressed a gentle kiss to her temple.

"No." Her leg rested between his thighs, and she felt the leap of renewed passion. Anticipation stirred deep inside her. "Why? What did you have in mind?"

"As if you didn't know," he chided, laughing softly. "Is it time for seconds?"

"You're insatiable," she said, rubbing her leg against his hardening erection.

"Horny, too." Laughing, he flipped onto his back, grasped her hips and settled her on top of him, over him, sheathing him. "It's now up to you, love. You may take a slow ride or a fast gallop."

Fully enjoying being in control, Krissy freely indulged her body, first in the former, then in the latter of his suggestions.

"Rand?" Krissy's voice was blurry after waking from a three-hour nap.

"Umph."

"Wake up." She lightly scraped her nails from his shoulder and down the length of his arm.

"Umm." He still sounded half-asleep. "That felt good. Do it again." Even half-asleep he was sexy.

"No." She laughed. "You like it too much."

He yawned, hugely. "If not for more of my patented brand of torture," he said, smothering another yawn. "What was so darned important you had to wake me."

"I'm hungry."

He opened one eye. "Well, I just offered . . ."

"For food," she interrupted, feigning impatience, which wasn't easy as she was grinning at him.

"Oh, that." He opened the other eye. "Is that all?"

"Well, no."

"Really?" He wiggled his eyebrows suggestively. "What else is bothering you? Anything I can help you with?"

"Yes." She was still smiling.

"Glad to be of service." He kissed her, with passion and obvious meaning.

Krissy loved it, but shoved at his chest, laughing when he came up for air. "I said not that." She hesitated, then clarified. "At least not yet."

Rand heaved a heartfelt, and obviously fake, sigh. "Okay, love, what's on your mind?"

"The Fourth of July."

"Huh?" He blinked. "What about it?"

"It's next week."

"So?"

"Well," she huffed. "What are we going to do to celebrate the holiday?"

"I . . ." He shook his head, as if to clear the cobwebs. "I don't know. I didn't know you wanted to celebrate it."

"Well, I do. I love the Fourth of July."

"Okay." He rolled his eyes to the ceiling, as though seeking guidance.

"I've always loved it," she said, offended by his expression.

"You're kind of goofy, you know that?" He grinned to take the sting from his remark.

It didn't work. "Goofy, am I?" she cried. "You're the one who wanted this . . . this . . . affair."

Rand shot into a sitting position; she suspected it was just so he could glare down at her.

"We are not having an affair, we are having a relationship." He came within a slim hair of shouting at her. "And I was teasing by calling you goofy, and dammit, you know it." He tossed the covers off of them both as though he meant business. "Get up."

"Why?" Krissy glared back at him.

"Because we are going to make a little trip to jewelers' row, where I'm going to put a diamond engagement ring big enough to choke a horse on your finger." He jumped from the bed, seriously agitated. "That will put the stamp of approved intent on our relationship."

Continuing to glare at him, Krissy didn't move. "Rand, I told you I didn't —"

"I know what you told me." He cut her off with the slicing movement of his hand. "Now, *I'm* telling *you.* I love you. I want to marry you. You said yes to me weeks ago. Now, haul your ass out of that bed and let's shower, dress and go make it official."

She blinked at him. "You're serious."

He heaved another, this time real, sigh. "Krissy, love, I am totally serious." Taking her hands, he drew her upright. "Krissy.

You're tearing me apart here. Please let me put my ring on your finger."

"Just the engagement ring," she said tremulously.

"Okay, just the engagement ring." He smiled, with a tinge of determination. "For now."

"On one, no, two conditions." She sounded every bit as determined.

He sighed again. "What are they?"

"First, we order something to eat from room service before we leave."

"All right. What else?"

She smiled, coaxingly. "While we're eating, we make plans for the Fourth of July."

Rand lost it. Doubling up with roaring laughter, he fell back onto the bed. While he was busy having an amusement fit over her requests, Krissy dashed into the bathroom and flicked the switch on the lock.

Moments later, he was pounding on the door, demanding she let him in.

"I'm going to take a quick shower," she shouted through the door. "In the meantime, call room service. I'll have a French dip sandwich and a baked potato. And order another bottle of that good cabernet."

"You'll pay for this, too, sweetheart," he

growled in mock warning, tacking on, "Later tonight."

"Oh, that meal was so good," Krissy said an hour or so later. She raised her glass to him. "Thank you."

"You're welcome." Rand also raised his glass, tipping it toward her. "But thanking me doesn't get you off the hook. You're still going to pay for locking me out."

"Promises, promises," she taunted. "So, let's get back to important stuff. What do you want to do to celebrate the Fourth. Any ideas?"

"I'll let you set the agenda. I haven't a clue what's available in this city."

"Oh my God, Rand," Krissy cried fervently. "We're in the birthplace of our country." A soft smile of remembrance touched her lips. "Years ago, the state had a motto and song that went, America starts here, in Pennsylvania. There have been a lot of different state mottoes since that, but I always loved that one best."

"Well, well, we really do learn something new every day," Rand said, his smile for her gentle and beautiful.

Krissy frowned in confusion. "What do you mean?"

"You are a dyed-in-the-wool patriot." He

gave her a tender smile. "You really do love this state."

Krissy nodded. "I really do love our country, most especially this state." Reaching across the narrow room service table, she grasped his hand. "Oh, Rand, you are in for a treat. An historical feast."

"Okay, I'm game. What's on the menu?"

"Well, to begin, next week is the yearly Welcome To Philadelphia celebration. There will be all kinds of festivities, lots of fireworks, at the museum, at the ball game. I don't know exactly how many. We'll go to Penn's Landing to watch the ones set off over the Delaware River."

"Sounds good, I —" he began.

"But that's not all," she interrupted. "We're going to visit Independence Hall, The Liberty Bell, the National Constitution Center, the Betsy Ross house, Elfreth's Alley . . ."

"Wait a minute." Rand held up his hand. "Why are we going to an alley?"

"It's not just any old alley, Rand," Krissy corrected him. "It's a block that has thirty-some houses, a lot of them built before the Revolution. It's located in the middle of the Old City and is the nation's oldest residential street. I'd guess that thousands of people have lived there and so far as I know, most of the homes are still occupied. But I think there's one that's kept open for tourists."

"You amaze me," Rand murmured in awe. "How do you know all this historical stuff?"

"I grew up here, even if it wasn't right here in Center City." Her smile was sly. "Besides, American history was my favorite subject in school."

He pushed back his chair and stood. "Okay, love. Let's get going." He circled to hold her chair.

"Rand, the festivities don't start till next week. Where do you think we're going?"

"To find a ring to slip on your finger." He turned to her, raising one eyebrow. "What? You thought I'd forget?"

He was such a darling. She raised up on tiptoe to give him a sweet, adoring kiss.

"What was that for?" he asked, his voice roughened with emotion.

"That was for you . . . being you."

"Ahhh, Krissy," he whispered, resting his forehead against hers. "I honestly, truly, do love you."

"And I honestly, truly, do love you back."

He jerked his head up. "Enough to marry me now?"

"Don't push it, lover," she said, wryly.

Rand laughed, grabbed her hand, and headed for the door.

CHAPTER 14

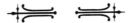

Jon drove Julia into the city late in the after-noon of the Friday of the Fourth of July week. They had booked a room at the same hotel she had stayed at in the spring, and where Krissy was still in residence in a lavish suite.

Julia and Jon had made love twice more that week. He had been passionate, the way he used to be with her, leading her to hope they were growing closer.

Yet, not once had Jon whispered to her he still loved her. Nor had he murmured how good they were together, in and out of bed. The unmentioned strain remained be-tween them.

"You know, this is the very same room I had in the spring?" Julia marveled, gazing at the number on the folder containing the computer key card the desk clerk handed to her.

"Yeah," Jon muttered, walking toward the bank of elevators. "The start of this whole business with Krissy and Laura," he said, after stepping into the empty car behind her.

"What business?" Julia frowned. "What are you talking about?"

Jon shrugged. "All of this running back and forth to meet for lunch, or the six of us meeting for the occasional dinner."

"I thought you enjoyed their company," Julia retorted, her voice sharp. "You said you did."

The car stopped at their floor. The doors hissed apart. Irritated, Julia swept past him along the corridor to their room.

He heaved a long-suffering sigh, which only succeeded in increasing her irritation. She was so agitated, she had to slide the card into the slot three times before the green light blinked, allowing her entrance into the room. She swung around to glare at him the moment he shut the door.

"What was that put-upon sigh all about?" she said, not even trying to conceal her anger. "Were you lying to me when you claimed to enjoy those evenings out?"

"No, of course not." Jon raked his hand through his hair. "I just meant, all that time spent together, and still you three feel a need to spend a week away."

The anger inside Julia expanded. It was

to the point of exploding from her mouth when a tap sounded on the door, followed by a call.

"Bellman."

Turning away, Julia strode to the wide window and gazed at the now familiar panoramic scene below. She managed a tight, sad smile for the statue of William Penn atop city hall. This time, she didn't greet the state's founder, aloud or silently.

"Thank you, sir, I hope you enjoy your stay." The voice of the bellman, and the gentle closing of the door as he departed, broke into her brooding thoughts.

Fat chance of that, Julia thought, grateful she and Jon would only be there that one night. She, Krissy and Laura were leaving for the shore after checking out tomorrow. Well, she and Jon would be checking out. Laura was driving in from New Jersey, and Rand would be staying in the suite.

"What is your problem with my spending a girls' week away, Jon?" she asked, her annoyance clear in the tightness of her voice. "You're away for days and at times a week several times each year."

"But that's for business," he snapped back. "Not for pleasure."

"Oh, give me a break." Julia made a rude

noise. Somewhere between a snort and a mocking laugh. "Are you actually trying to tell me you never have a good time at those conferences and seminars? You never meet up with old friends, go out to eat, have a few drinks, laugh and enjoy yourself?" Before he could respond, she continued scathingly, "Do you honestly take me for that big a fool?"

"No!" Jon exclaimed in denial. "Dammit, Julia, you know full well I have always treated you and your intelligence with respect, and I have never so much as given a thought to taking you for a fool."

"Then why do you resent my going away with my oldest and dearest friends?" On a roll, Julia was not about to stop, even though he opened his mouth to reply. "You have left me on my own so often, holding down the fort. First I was running after kids, now I run the kids around to all their games and classes. It's exhausting."

"Julia." Jon's tone held a plea. "I know you've been a model doctor's wife, but you did know I was a doctor before you married me."

Julia threw her hands up. "I'm not complaining about your profession, Jon. Have I ever? I'm just saying, you're being unfair by objecting to my being away. All I want to know is . . . why?"

"I'll be alone." Simple and straightforward.

"Oh, Lord!" Julia didn't know whether to laugh or cry. "I've been alone for most of our married life. Which, in case you don't realize it, means *you* weren't there. And now, with the Ems in Florida, I'd be almost completely alone, as I have been for the past week."

Jon's shoulders drooped a bit. "What do you want from me, Julia? Should I trim back my schedule to spend more time with you and the girls? What?"

"Oh, good grief. All this over a lousy week at the shore?" Shaking her head, Julia caught sight of the desk clock. "We don't have time for this discussion, Jon. We need to get ready to meet the others for dinner."

"But," he said, halting her as she scooped up her flight bag and started for the bathroom. "We are going to continue this discussion when you get home."

"Oh, you'd better believe we are." Julia was amazed by the hard note in her tone. "An in-depth discussion between you and me is long overdue."

She zipped into the bathroom before he

could utter one word of either agreement or protest.

Dinner was . . . different.

Instead of the steady stream of conversation flying back and forth between the three couples, Julia, Krissy and Laura rattled away almost nonstop about their getaway trip, hardly taking time to consume their meals.

The men, on the other hand, concentrated on their food, offering only desultory comments every so often.

At one point, Krissy briefly glanced from one male to the other, then looked at Julia and Laura, rolled her eyes and mouthed the word *pitiful.*

Naturally, the three women proceeded to give way to an attack of the giggles. That got the men's attention.

"What's the joke?" Rand asked.

"Yeah, let us in on it," Drew added.

"We could use a laugh, too," Jon agreed.

Krissy waved one hand airily. "Oh, it's just silly girl talk. You wouldn't understand."

Of course, her remark set off Julia and Laura again. Both women covered their mouth to stifle more giggles.

Smiling indulgently, Rand gazed in turn

at Jon and Drew. "Women. Will any of us ever understand them?"

"Isn't that what I just said?" Krissy piped in, not giving the other two men time to answer.

Julia and Laura were off and running again with the giggles, and this time Krissy joined in.

"You know, maybe it's a good thing these three are going away for a week," Rand observed. "Get all this giddiness out of their systems."

"I sincerely hope so," Jon drawled, his smile the first genuine one of the evening.

"Ditto." Drew didn't smile.

But Laura did. The smile she gave Drew was so saccharine, it was blatantly phony. "Give it a rest, Drew," she said, her voice edgy.

Oh, boy, Julia thought, eyeing the couple. Things obviously are not all rosy in the Hartline marriage. Not that she blamed Laura for a minute, not if she was right about Drew repeatedly cheating on her.

"Well, then," Krissy said, her tone light and bubbly in an attempt to ease the tense table. "Is everybody ready for dessert?"

She was answered with negatives from all sides.

"All right." She soldiered on brightly, "More wine? Coffee, anyone?"

"I'll have more wine," Laura said, defiance blazing from her eyes as she glared at Drew.

"So have more." He glared back at her. "And so will I. No, I'll have a whiskey and soda."

Rand and Jon exchanged meaningful glances.

Krissy bit her lip.

Julia swallowed a groan. Wonderful. What a terrific way for the evening to end.

Fortunately, after Laura and Drew had had their rebellious drinks, and the other four had finished the coffee none of them obviously wanted, they called it a night.

"Okay, kids," Krissy said while they stood outside waiting for the car to pick them up. "The limo heads south tomorrow morning at eleven-thirty." She grinned. "Be there or be square."

Julia groaned aloud. "That expression is so ancient, even its mold has grown mold."

The expected limo glided to the curb and the six of them piled in.

"What's with Laura and Drew?" Jon asked, double-locking the hotel room door.

Julia was tempted to shrug as if to say,

beats me, but a sudden thought changed her mind. Telling him the truth just might hit home.

"Laura is certain Drew's cheating on her and has been for some time," she said, looking him straight in the eyes. "And I think she's pretty fed up with it . . . and him."

"Really?" Jon didn't appear at all surprised. "I don't doubt she's right."

Julia was startled. "Do you know something?"

He shook his head. "Not anything definite. But I've seen the way he checks out every attractive woman who happens to pass by his line of vision." His smile was all-knowing, all-masculine. "When Laura appeared not to be noticing, of course. Apparently, she noticed more than he knew."

"Not apparently," Julia corrected him, frustrated by his lack of display of any guilt or dismay. "Obviously she has noticed everything."

"Ummm." He nodded and removed his suit jacket and tie. "I'd say their marriage is in trouble." He sauntered to the bathroom. "You don't mind if I go first, do you? I'll only be a minute."

Would it matter if she did? Julia wondered, as he closed the door after him.

Jon was in bed by the time she left the bathroom, her face shiny and clear of makeup, her teeth brushed, her body clad in a summer nightgown of thin cotton. He looked out of it and she assumed he was asleep.

She was wrong. He turned to her as she slipped beneath the covers, one arm circling her waist to turn her on her side, draw her against him. He was naked, ready, his hard erection pressing into her.

"Jon . . . ?"

He silenced her with a kiss. Although it started soft and gentle, within seconds his mouth grew restless, desperate, hot as his body. At first she went still, but then his tongue thrust into her mouth. Need stirred inside Julia, desire igniting a hungry urge to respond.

His hands moved over her body, touching, teasing, exploring. His mouth followed the path of his hands, his tongue laving every inch of her . . . *every inch!*

Julia went rigid with shock. Jon had never . . . Her thoughts dissolved from the liquid fire racing through her from her core to her whirling brain. Instinctively she arched into the pleasure of his ministrations. Her fingers curled, grasping onto the sheet beneath her writhing body.

Tension coiled inside, tighter, tighter, until Julia, releasing the sheet to grasp his head, nearly cried aloud at the incredible sensations. Then he stopped, lifting his head to stare into her face, as though finding pleasure in her expression of passion strained to the limit.

"Jon . . . what?"

"Not yet," he said, in a soft unfamiliar rasp.

Grabbing her hips in his hands, he raised her up and plunged into her. He continued to thrust, deeper and deeper, his fingers digging into the tender flesh of her bottom. Julia gasped at his abandoned roughness, his wildness.

Within moments her breath became labored. Then a surge of wildness overtook *her.* Clinging to his hips, she arched to meet his every thrust. *She* was as much the aggressor as Jon, matching his roughness and abandonment.

Higher and higher the tension spiraled. Then it shattered, flinging her into a pulsating, shimmering orgasm unlike anything she had ever experienced before.

A scream rose in her throat. Jon's mouth latched on to hers, swallowing her scream as, shuddering with his own racking orgasm, his outcry echoed inside her head.

For the very first time ever, Julia drifted off to sleep before making a trip to the bathroom to clean herself. She woke several hours later. Two realizations hit her one after another. Jon was dead to the world, snoring beside her. And she was still wearing her nightgown, bunched up to her neck. He had been in such a frenzied hurry, he hadn't taken the time needed to remove it.

Julia felt sweaty and sticky. The cool air-conditioned air chilled her uncovered body.

She also felt used. To the bone. Satisfied, maybe even more so, but used, nevertheless. She didn't like the feeling. If Jon had murmured words of love to her while arousing her as never before, Julia knew she would be feeling utterly content, utterly loved by her husband.

But Jon hadn't murmured those words. He hadn't murmured anything other than "Not yet."

Not yet. The words rang in her head. Not yet. As if he were speaking not to his wife but to any woman who had happened to be beneath his pounding body.

Shivering from the outer chill, and a deeper inner coldness, Julia dragged her tired body from the bed to stand under a beating hot shower. The very idea of feeling somehow dirtied by her husband's lovemaking made her sick to her stomach.

Thank heavens she had agreed to go to the shore for a week with Krissy and Laura, Julia thought, pulling on a clean nightgown that didn't smell of raw sex.

Her escape couldn't come soon enough.

CHAPTER 15

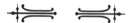

Julia sighed with relief as she stepped off the elevator to see Krissy and Laura already in the lobby. They were alone; neither Rand nor Drew were with them.

Julia was also alone, as Jon had left early that morning to drive back to Hershey to be in his office for his first appointment.

They had shared a mostly quiet breakfast, speaking sporadically about nothing of any importance.

But the day was coming when they would be having a very important discussion. Either that or a knock-down, drag-out argument. Julia could only hope it wouldn't come to that.

"Here she is," Krissy said, spying Julia walking toward them, a carry-on strap over her shoulder and pulling a large wheeled suitcase behind.

Standing with her back to Julia, Laura spun around, a wide smile of greeting on her lips. "Hi," she called, a happy note in her voice.

"Hi," Julia responded, her own smile as bright as the others, as if she didn't have a care in the world. "Have I kept you waiting long?"

"Nope, we both just got here." Laura glanced out through the wide glass doors. "Matter of fact, the car is pulling up now." She looked at her watch. "Exactly on time."

Within minutes the driver and the doorman had their bags stashed, and the three women were ensconced comfortably in the long, luxurious limo.

A thermos of hot coffee and a napkin-draped tray of cookies and small pastries was waiting for them. Between sipping and nibbling, they chatted all through the hour-and-fifteen-minute drive. Not one of them noticed the passing scenery or the passage of time, and so were surprised and delighted when the driver pulled the car into the Realtor's parking lot.

The driver left the car and went into the office. Moments later he returned with a fortyish pleasant-looking man in tow. The driver opened the door closest to Krissy.

"Ms. Trzcinski?" the man asked, leaning down to peer into the car.

"Krissy," she corrected, extending her hand. "Nice to meet you, Dan."

"Nice to meet you." Dan grasped her hand, giving her an attractive smile.

"I'd like you to meet my dearest friends," Krissy said, pointing in turn to the others. "Julia Langston and Laura Hartline. Julia, Laura, this is Dan Albright."

Pleasantries were exchanged along with handshaking. Dan handed Krissy a ring of door keys and a large white envelope. After he told her to give him a call if there were any questions or problems, they were on their way once more.

"Ohmigosh!" Laura exclaimed, as the driver turned the long car onto a familiar street. "Look at how everything has changed around here. These are nearly all new buildings."

"And every one of them looks expensive," Julia murmured, wondering what in heaven's name Krissy had paid to stay in the three-story building where the car had stopped. "Krissy, what did you have to pay for this place?"

Krissy gave a careless wave of her slender, still ringless left hand. "Don't worry about it. It was nothing."

Nothing, Julia repeated to herself. Right. Knowing better than to argue with her friend, she merely rolled her eyes at Laura as they followed in Krissy's wake.

There was an elevator — an elevator, of all things — in the three-story apartment building. Julia recalled running up the four flights of stairs at the place they'd once stayed when the three of them were younger . . . much younger.

"An elevator?" she murmured, raising her eyebrows.

"Better be." Krissy inserted one of the keys into a slot next to the lift. "It's the only way to get into the place, other than the fire escape in the back, which also can only be opened with a key," she airily explained.

"Wait," Julia said, a sudden realization striking her as the single door slid closed. "What about our bags?"

"Don't worry, hon," Krissy said, touching the button for the third floor. "Tim will take care of everything." She flashed a brilliant smile. "That's why he receives an exorbitant salary."

Of course, Julia thought with amusement. Why didn't I think of that?

The elevator came to a stop and opened to reveal a small landing with a door on its far side.

"Okay," Krissy said, first to step out of

the car. Keys jangled on the ring as she selected another and headed for the door. "Let's see what this place looks like."

"You haven't seen it?" Julia asked.

"Well, of course not," Krissy answered, inserting the key in the lock. "When would I have gotten down here?" She turned the key and opened the door. "I only finished shooting a little over a week ago." Stepping aside, she waved them inside. "Home away from home for a week."

"Holy shit!" Laura cried, immediately clamping a hand over her mouth as she walked into the spacious living room. "Just look at the size of this place!"

It wasn't big; it was huge. The layout was open, the living room flowing into a dining room with a table and eight chairs. Both rooms had wide windows and glass sliding doors onto a long deck, which faced the boardwalk and the ocean beyond.

"Will you look at that view," Julia murmured in a tone of appreciative awe.

"Holy . . . ah . . . moley," Laura murmured from beside her.

"Well," Krissy said in pleased satisfaction. "Dan was right. He said the view was great."

"He was damned straight on that," Laura said. She turned suddenly, her eyes going wide. "Hey, we forgot to stop at the liquor store on our way here," she said, frowning her disappointment.

Laughing, Krissy shook her head at Laura. "Not to worry, Tim has a case of champagne in the car."

Julia gave an exaggerated arch of her eyebrows. "Champagne, yet. I'll drink to that."

"You'd better," Krissy said, grinning. "Or Laura and I will spend every night smashed."

Laura giggled. "I still might. I don't handle alcohol very well."

"We know."

"We have witnessed it."

Julia and Krissy exchanged smiles.

There was a light tap at the door.

"Oh, Tim!" Krissy said, hurrying to let the driver in.

Incredibly, he had managed to cram all the luggage, the champagne and himself into the elevator. "Where would you like me to put the bags and wine, Krissy?"

Neither Julia nor Laura were surprised by the man using Krissy's first name, any more than they had been surprised to hear Dan use it. Krissy had always disliked a formal address, claiming it sounded too subservient to her.

"Just set them down near the hallway,

Tim," she said. "We can manage to drag them to our rooms once we've decided which rooms we want. We'll take care of the wine later."

"Okay." He set the cases down near the archway to the hall, then straightened. "Is that all for now?"

"Yes, thank you," she answered, bestowing a lovely smile on him. "You can head back to Philly."

He frowned. "But what if you need a car?"

"I'll call a cab."

"Well . . ." He was still unsure. "If you say so. But," he quickly added, "you will call me if you need me?"

"Yes, yes," Krissy said, shooing him away with a wave. "Go home and spend the weekend with your wife and kids . . . with pay."

"You are a very nice person, Krissy," Julia said in all seriousness after Tim had left.

She tossed her head, flipping the mane of red hair she had pulled back into a loose ponytail. "Well, thank you," she said, pleased and smiling. "I figure, why not be nice to people, it doesn't cost anything."

"Neither does being gruff or impatient or haughty," Laura pointed out. "Like a lot of people."

"Ahhh, but it does," Krissy said, grabbing the handle of her case and leading off down the hallway. "It can cost you in friends or even potential friends." She smiled over her shoulder. "Now, let's fight over who gets what room."

No fight was needed. There were three bedrooms, two large, the other larger. All three had private baths and walk-in closets. Julia and Laura agreed at once the larger, master bedroom should be Krissy's since she had paid for the condo.

All the rooms were decorated with a sea-side motif, the pictures on the walls, the bric-a-brac set on tables. Though they had only caught a glimpse of the kitchen, Julia presumed the same decor theme carried through there, as well.

Laura chose the bedroom with pink-and-white walls and furnishings. Julia was left with the room in sunny yellow and white. She didn't mind. In fact she loved it, as the colors seemed to fairly shout *summer* at the shore.

After putting her clothes in the closet and dresser drawers, Julia stashed her suitcase and carry-on and headed out to explore her home away from home for the next week. Krissy and Laura were standing together near the end of the hallway, gazing into another room.

"Hey, look at this," Laura said to Julia as she joined them. She flicked a hand to the side. "A powder room there, close to the living room."

Julia took a quick peek into the room, as Laura continued, "And a laundry room in here, complete with washer, dryer and a rack for us to hang our delicates to dry."

"Ummm," Julia hummed, smiling at her two friends. "And then some, I'd say."

"You don't have a washer and dryer?" Krissy cried, in feigned horror.

"Or a drying rack?"

"Well, naturally," Julia drawled, playing along. "But not with pictures of the ocean and seabirds on the walls."

"Oh, poor darling," Krissy commiserated. "How terrible for you. Come with me. I'll pour a glass of wine for you to soothe your frazzled nerves."

Laura faked a shudder. "Warm champagne?"

Krissy threw her "the look." "I assure you, Laura, this place has all the amenities, even, brace yourself, a refrigerator with an ice maker." She arched one brow dramatically. "You have something against ice in your champagne?"

"Heck no," Laura said, as Julia laughed,

tempting her to laugh along. "I'll take it any way you serve it."

Laughing together like old times, the three friends strolled through the living and dining rooms.

The dining room opened into a large kitchen. An island work surface stood in the middle of the floor with four high stools set before it. All the counter surfaces were gray slate. The appliances and many cabinets were gleaming white. The walls were painted a shade between sea-green and blue.

"Beautiful," Julia said, her smile soft for Krissy. "Every thing is simply beautiful. Thank you so much for inviting me to share this with you."

"And I want to add my thanks, too," Laura said, gazing around her as if transfixed. "I'd ask how much this gorgeous place cost you . . . but I'm afraid I'd faint at the answer."

"Then I won't tell you," Krissy said, turning to go for the wine. "C'mon, ladies, help me lug the booze into the kitchen. A full glass will be your reward."

The wine lugged, Laura opened the fridge, only to stare inside in disbelief. "Oh, nurse, I'm worse," she muttered. "Who stocked the fridge?"

"I asked Dan to have it loaded for me," Krissy said. "I thought we wouldn't want to eat out all the time."

"Good thinking," Julia said, glad they wouldn't have to go out for coffee first thing in the morning.

Ice rattled into champagne flutes. The cork made a soft pop. Golden liquid flowed over the ice to the top of the glass rims. When all three glasses were full, they turned as one and walked onto the deck, gazing out at the ocean.

"Gee it's good to be here, together again," Laura said, softly sighing.

"Yes." Krissy's sigh echoed hers.

Julia deeply inhaled. "The scent of the ocean, the surf rushing to shore, the cry of the gulls." She smiled at the other two. "It's almost like coming home."

In peaceful silence they sipped their wine.

The days seemed to fly by. The weather was perfect. Each sunny morning they went to the beach where Julia and Laura played tag with the waves and Krissy spent most of the time beneath a hired beach umbrella.

At noon they left the beach to have lunch, either to make it back at the condo or, more often than not, to grab pizza at Mack and Manco's.

After lunch they spent some time strolling the boardwalk. They'd go in and out of the shops, buying trinkets they really had no use for but couldn't resist.

They also bought fudge. The best fudge Julia had ever tasted. They ate it every night as they sipped their wine while sitting on the deck, soaking up the atmosphere.

At one point, Laura asked point blank, "What's the deal with you and Rand, Krissy? Are you two engaged or not?"

"We are," she admitted.

"So, why no ring?" Julia asked. "I distinctly remember Rand saying there would be a ring."

"I selected one. It had to be sized to fit me," Krissy explained. "Rand could pick it up this week."

"I'll bet it's huge!" Laura said.

"I'll bet it's beautiful," Julia said with a smile.

Krissy laughed. "You're both right."

Some evenings, after showering and getting into comfortable clothes, they'd eat in. At those times they chattered away late into the night, seemingly never able to exhaust their conversations.

Other nights they ate out at local restaurants, chattering away over the table, and after they returned to the condo. One evening they cabbed it to Atlantic City for dinner and a bit of gambling.

"It's not Vegas," Krissy observed, gazing around her. "But it's not bad, either."

"Noisy."

"And glitzy."

Krissy gazed at them with a frown. "It's a casino. It's supposed to be noisy and . . . not glitzy, glamorous."

"Yeah, yeah," Laura chided. "Let's find a nice restaurant. I'm starving."

Julia and Laura both lost a little money playing the slots. Krissy, naturally, won a little playing blackjack. All in all, they had a lovely evening out.

Their last evening they decided to stay in and just hang together, continuing their never-ending conversations. They called for takeout sandwiches and ate them with their wine. Lots of wine. Only this time, the conversation took a more serious turn.

After her second glass of wine, Laura sighed, her expression dejected as she refilled her glass. "You know, I hate the idea of this week ending, it's been so relaxing." She glanced from Julia to Krissy, a sad smile shadowing her lips. "I wish we could stay here forever."

Julia gave her a searching look. "What's wrong? Why don't you want to go home?"

"Is it Drew?" Krissy said, narrowing her eyes.

"Who else?" Laura shrugged. "I'm so sick of his screwing around." This time, her smile was apologetic. "After being with you two all week, hearing about your normal lives. Your happiness . . . I . . ."

"Ahhh . . . wait a minute, Laura," Julia inserted. "Whatever made you think my life was all roses?"

Laura gulped a swallow of wine before asking in disbelief, "Don't tell me you and Jon have problems."

"Hon, no one is perfect. Everybody has problems. Jon and I are no exception."

"Yeah, domestic ones, but . . ."

"But nothing," Julia cut in. "Jon and I have been having personal problems for several years now — ever since Emily was thrown from her horse." She went on to explain her feelings about resenting Jon.

Krissy said, "I couldn't imagine the pressure and responsibility on a surgeon under those conditions. No wonder he wouldn't perform the surgery."

"I can't believe you expected him to do

the surgery," Laura chimed in.

"Well, I did. I begged him to do it," Julia defended herself. "I know in my heart and mind, Jon is the best, and I trusted him implicitly . . . then."

"Then?" Krissy asked, picking up on Julia's slight hesitation. "What's happened since then to change your mind?"

"I think he might be involved with his nurse practitioner."

"Oh, shit, not Jon, too?" Laura muttered.

"Are you sure?" Krissy said.

"Well, he has admitted to having kissed her on several occasions. What would you think?"

"I'd think he was screwing around," Laura said in disgust. "Looks like the only really happy one here is Krissy. Rand is obviously crazy about her."

Krissy suddenly burst out crying.

"What's the matter?" Laura asked, alarmed. "What did I say?" She looked at Julia for help.

As alarmed as Laura, Julia looked every bit as puzzled. "Krissy, honey, what's wrong?"

Krissy was still weeping. Sitting closest to a box of tissues, Laura handed one to her. "Please, Krissy," she pleaded. "Tell us what's wrong. Why are you crying?"

"I . . . I'm . . . so damned . . . scared," Krissy said between sobbing breaths.

"Scared?" Julia and Laura said in unison, exchanging confused looks.

"Scared of what?" Julia asked.

"My mother —" Krissy broke off to blow her nose.

"Your mother?" Now Julia was more than confused, she was concerned for Krissy's state of inebriation. "Hon, I think maybe you've had enough wine."

"No . . . no, you don't understand," Krissy said, drawing a deep breath. "I . . . I found a lump. . . ." She sniffed. "In my breast . . . I . . . I'm afraid, so afraid. You both know how horribly my mother suffered."

"Oh, Krissy," Julia said, getting up to go to her, sitting next to her on the love seat. She put her arm around Krissy's shoulders. On the other side, Laura did the same. "How long has it been since you felt it?"

"A couple months. Late winter, early spring." Krissy shook her head. "I'm not sure anymore."

Julia and Laura frowned in concern at each other over Krissy's bent head.

"What did your doctor say about it?" Laura asked.

"Did he perform a biopsy?" Julia said.

"No." Krissy again shook her head. "I . . . haven't seen a doctor."

"Haven't seen one?" Julia was stunned. "What did Rand have to say about that?"

Krissy lowered her head, mumbling, "He doesn't know about the lump."

"You're engaged to the man and didn't tell him?" Julia stared at her in disbelief.

"Krissy, are you crazy?" Laura demanded. "You must tell Rand, and you must see a doctor."

"But . . ." she began.

"No buts," Julia insisted. "Krissy, you know damned well the sooner a diagnosis is made the better."

"A diagnosis!" Krissy cried frantically. "We all know what a diagnosis and tests will show. Don't we?"

"Oh, Krissy!" Laura said in frustration.

"We don't know anything of the kind," Julia said, her voice tight with her own fear. "You've got to see a doctor."

"My doctor's in California," Krissy came close to shouting. "I'd have no idea who to go to, who to trust in Philly."

"Well, Jon will know," Julia said, getting up to fetch her cell phone. "And I'm calling him right now."

"But . . ."

"She already said no buts, Krissy," Laura said. "Now shut up and don't argue. If you won't take care of yourself, we'll do it for you."

Jon answered on the second ring. "Hello, Julia?" he said, over some background noise.

"Where are you?" she asked, skipping a greeting.

"I'm having a late dinner in a sports bar," he explained. "There's a ball game blaring from a half dozen TVs."

"Oh." Just couldn't help but wonder who might be with him. But she didn't have time to ask.

"Are you all right?" Jon said, sounding concerned.

"Yes, I am," she assured him. "It's Krissy, she needs your help."

"In what way?" Now he sounded confused.

"She discovered a lump in her breast a couple of months ago." She exhaled a quick sigh. "She hasn't seen a doctor yet."

"What?" He shouted over the background noise. "Why in the hell not?"

She winced. "I know how you feel. She says her doctor is in California and she doesn't know who to trust in Philly. I told her you would know of a good one."

"Of course I do. Jesus, Julia," he went on, impatiently. "After losing her mother, you'd think Krissy would know better than to let this go."

"She's terrified, Jon," she said softly.

"Yes," he replied gently. The friend and doctor speaking. "I understand. I know just the person. A woman at the University of Pennsylvania hospital. I'll give her a call tomorrow before I leave for Philly. Do you have any idea what time you'll be leaving to come back?"

"The car will be here at eleven," she said. "We have to be out of here by noon. We're all packed and ready."

"Okay, I'll see you when you get in." He hesitated, then went on, "Julia . . . I missed you."

She felt a tightness in her throat. "I missed you, too, Jon," she said, just then realizing how much she had missed him, and for how long.

CHAPTER 16

Krissy was calm the next day, almost too calm. Julia had a feeling she was holding herself together by sheer willpower, a determination not to fall apart again.

Her eyes were a little puffy, but other than that, Krissy looked as beautiful as ever. While Julia had always admired her friend's beauty as well as her seemingly unfailing spirit, her high regard went up a notch at the way Krissy had imposed control on herself after Julia related Jon's plan.

She just couldn't believe Krissy might have to go through what her mother had suffered. By the tense concern evident on Laura's face, she couldn't believe it either.

As promised, Jon was at the hotel waiting for them when they arrived. He, along with Rand and Drew, were in Krissy's suite. He hadn't said a word to Rand, either about Krissy's lump or the appointment he had made for her.

Krissy breezed into the suite as if she

hadn't a care in the world. Almost immediately Rand seemed to know something wasn't right.

"Krissy, what's wrong?" Rand asked, frowning as he moved to her. "You've been crying."

Krissy, biting her lip, didn't answer fast enough. Rand turned to confront Julia and Laura. "Krissy never cries. Something happened." His usually pleasant voice was hard, demanding. "What was it?"

"Rand, stay calm, and let Krissy speak." Jon's voice was every bit as hard as Rand's had been.

"But . . . dammit! I want . . ."

Krissy halted Rand's agitated reply with a touch of her hand on his. "It's all right. I had too much wine last night and fell apart. Bawling like a baby."

"Why?" His tone was confused and anxious. "What made you cry?"

Wetting her lips, Krissy tried another smile; it was shaky at best. "I found a lump in my breast," she blurted out so quickly the words ran together. "And I'm scared."

He was instantly concerned. "What did your doctor say? How do we handle it?"

His use of the word *we* instantly endeared him to Julia, and if their expressions were any indication, to Jon and Laura.

234

Drew appeared baffled, and a bit impatient.

Julia immediately felt impatient with him.

"I haven't seen a doctor," Krissy admitted.

"What?" Rand asked in disbelief. "Krissy . . ."

"My mother died from breast cancer, Rand," Krissy shouted him down. "I watched her die. I'm terrified."

"Oh, sweetheart," Rand murmured, gently drawing her into his arms. "You have to see a doctor."

"Which is exactly what she's going to do in —" Jon paused to glance at his watch "— exactly an hour and a half. I'll be going with her."

"Like hell," Rand protested. "I'll be with her."

"You got me an appointment on a Saturday?" Krissy said, obviously surprised.

Jon nodded. "Yes. I thought I'd go with you, introduce you to her —" He was again cut off.

"It's a woman?" Krissy sounded delighted.

"Yes, and a well-respected oncologist. She did part of her residency at Hershey. That's where I met her. Since then, she has made a real name for herself in the field of breast cancer. She works out of the University of Pennsylvania Hospital."

"Fine," Rand inserted. "I'm still going with you."

An hour later Jon, Krissy and Rand left for Krissy's appointment. Laura wanted to wait with Julia in her and Jon's room, but Drew insisted they go pick up their kids before heading home. Obviously annoyed, but just as obviously not wanting a scene, Laura agreed, insisting Krissy call her as soon as she had any news.

Julia went to the room Jon had booked for them. As they were staying only the one night, she didn't bother to unpack anything but her cosmetics case, a nightgown and the clothing she planned to wear home. With nothing to keep her physically busy, her mind kept itself occupied worrying about Krissy's health and the state of her own marriage.

An attempt to distract herself by watching TV didn't work. She was left to fidget, surfing the channels for hours.

Laura was furious with Drew, and let him know it as soon as they were out of the worst of the Center City traffic.

"What's wrong with you?" she said, her

voice tight with anger. "Krissy's one of my dearest friends and you know it. I wanted to stay, be there for her when she got back from the doctor, just in case the news wasn't good."

"I'm sorry about that, and Krissy's problem," he defended himself, sounding more put-upon than sorry. "But I have a golf date for later this afternoon with some guys from the office and I wanted to get you and the kids home first."

"A golf game?" Laura flashed a narrow-eyed glance at him. "You made a date to play golf the same day I come home after a week away?"

"Well, why not?" Now Drew sounded self-righteous and defensive. "You had a seven day vacation. Why shouldn't I play golf this afternoon?"

Why indeed? Laura thought, bitterness causing a sour taste in her mouth. Perish the thought he'd want to spend the afternoon and evening with his wife and kids, whom he hadn't seen in a week.

"I had thought we might pick up the kids and stop somewhere for dinner together before going home," she said, a whiff of the bitterness tainting her voice.

"Couldn't anyway," he returned with a shrug. "The guys and I agreed to play until dark, then have dinner at the club."

Ahhh, yes, the country club he had joined mere days after they had moved into the area. He had explained to Laura that it was a prestige thing, befitting his new position. At the time, if she hadn't been so damned disgusted by the amount of money he had blown joining the club, she might have laughed in his smug, self-satisfied face.

Laura had never been inside the club, even though she knew she very likely would have to go there with Drew at some time or other. She hadn't been outside the club either, certainly not for the tennis courts, and not even the club's pool. Their development had a community pool with very reasonable yearly membership dues.

"You don't mind, do you?" Drew's voice carried a thread of belligerence. "I haven't played all week."

Poor baby. And why hadn't he played all week? He had been on his own, she knew from calling the kids all week. Drew Jr. had told her he hadn't seen much of his dad, as he was working late most evenings.

Yeah. Right. Laura mentally sneered. She didn't believe a word he said anymore. He was lying through his teeth, thus the attitude. Although he might well be going to play, then have dinner, she felt positive he hadn't worked late the previous week.

Laura was tempted to call him on it, but swallowed the urge. What good would it do? He'd only deny it.

"No," she finally answered. "I don't mind."

Laura went still inside the moment the words were out of her mouth, the instant the realization dawned on her that she really didn't mind. In fact, she didn't care if he never came home. It would make her life much simpler.

"Well?" Julia said, jumping out of the chair when Jon walked into the room. "What did the doctor say?"

"Exactly what I expected her to say." Motioning for her to sit down again, he dropped onto the love seat facing the TV. "She examined Krissy, felt the lump, and wants her to have an ultrasound first, then probably a biopsy."

Julia sighed. "Of course she does." She sat facing him. "I should have realized she'd order some tests."

Jon nodded. "Thing is, she didn't seem too concerned. Probably to relax Krissy."

"Did it work?"

Jon smiled. "Julia, you know Krissy better

than that. You know it didn't work." He raked a hand through his hair. "She's convinced herself that she's going to repeat her mother's experience. Chemo, radiation and a painful death."

Julia bit her lip. "Is that what you believe?"

He seemed genuinely shocked. "I think nothing of the sort. It's been some time since Krissy's mother lost her life to cancer. A lot has changed. There are so many more advanced treatments. No, maybe Krissy has written herself off, but I sure as hell haven't."

Julia felt relieved and comforted. Sometimes it did pay to have a doctor in the family.

She was at once ashamed and sorry for having the bitter-sounding thought. Just because he had refused to operate on Emily didn't change the fact that Jon was an excellent physician and surgeon. Laura knew that full well. She had to somehow, in some way, get over this lingering resentment. She had known from day one that physicians, especially surgeons, felt too emotionally involved to treat members of their immediate family. And yet she persisted in this . . .

"She wants us to get together for dinner."

"What?" Julia blinked, grateful for the interruption of her self-chastising musings. "I'm sorry, I was off into my own thoughts. What did you say?"

"I said, Krissy would like us to get together with her and Rand for dinner this evening."

"Oh. Would you like to have dinner with them?"

He shrugged. "Sure, why not? We have to eat, and I enjoy their company. She suggested having dinner at the restaurant here in the hotel, which suits me. We can make it an early night since we'll be leaving fairly early in the morning. Or have you forgotten we have to pick up the girls at the airport in Harrisburg early tomorrow afternoon?"

"No, of course I didn't forget," Laura lied, for in truth, with all the trauma about Krissy, she had completely forgotten. Feeling even worse, like an uncaring mother, she quickly changed the subject. "What time does she want to meet?"

"Six. She said to give her a call if it doesn't suit. Otherwise, we're supposed to meet them at the restaurant at six. Okay?"

"Fine." A yawn caught her off guard and she raised a hand to her mouth just in time to cover another one.

"Tired?"

Julia sighed. "Yes. We were up late and . . . well, we all had a little too much wine," she explained. "And we all had a crying jag, not just Krissy." She offered him an apologetic smile. "If you don't mind, I think I'll lie down for a little while, have a nap."

"No, I don't mind." Jon hesitated, as if unsure of whether he wanted to continue. "I didn't sleep well either. Would . . . er . . . you mind if I joined you?"

For a moment, Julia was speechless. He was asking her permission to share the bed with her? Incredible. Was he also hoping for some . . .

"It's been a week, Julia," he softly reminded her.

Yes, he was hoping for some . . . She swallowed a sigh, wondering if he was also anticipating a repeat of the passion they'd shared a week before.

What else could she say but, "No, of course, I don't mind."

This time their lovemaking was different, a little different from last time. Jon whispered three words to her before arousing her body to the point of mindless abandonment.

"I missed you."

When it was over Julia felt herself stiffening up. She longed for words of love, for the true closeness they had once shared.

"What's wrong, Julia?" Jon said, concern clear in his tone.

Too spent and tired to go into any lengthy discussions, she grabbed at the most obvious excuse.

"I'm so scared for Krissy."

Holding her, he again murmured reassurances. Eventually, exhausted, they both did grow quiet and settle in for a nap.

Several floors above Julia and Jon's room, Krissy and Rand were also in their bed.

Softly weeping within the cradle of Rand's arms, Krissy moved back to look into his face. "I won't hold you to our engagement, knowing what's ahead."

Rand shot up onto one elbow to glare down at her. "Dammit, Krissy, stop talking like that. You don't know what's ahead. You'll have the tests the doctor ordered and then we'll see. Cancer is not a death sentence."

"But —" she began to say.

"But nothing," he cut her off, his anger evident as he grabbed a small black box from the night table. He took a large diamond ring from inside and put it on

Krissy's finger. "I picked the ring up from the jeweler. Now wear it."

"Rand, please, I . . ." she tried again.

"No." He shook his head, quick, sharp. "I'm holding you to our engagement. And I won't listen to another word about it. You are going to marry me, Krissy."

"Rand." She sniffed, tears running down her temples.

"What?" He reached across her to pull a handful of tissues from the box on the nightstand.

"You love my breasts." Still sniffling, she dabbed at the tears before blowing her nose.

"Yeah, so?" He looked baffled.

"I might lose them." Her voice was loud, scared. Tears spilled over her lids again; she mopped them up.

"I know that." He shook his head in disbelief. "Then again, you might not. Either way, what does that have to do with our engagement?"

"You love them . . ." She sniffed louder, and shuddered. "And if I lose them . . ." Her voice cracked.

"Oh, for Christ's sake, Krissy." Rand's voice was raw, his tone more a prayer than a curse. "Your breasts are beautiful. And, yes, I love them. They are a beautiful part of you, but they are only one part . . . not you. I love you, sweetheart, the person you are. And I'll go on loving you, with or without your gorgeous breasts."

Now Krissy was sobbing. "Oh, Rand, I love you, too, love you so much I was afraid of losing you if . . ."

He cradled her closer to him. "You're not going to lose me, sweetheart. I'm here to stay . . . for the long haul." Bending his head he gifted her with a tender kiss. "Get used to it."

"That's what scared me," Krissy admitted. "I *was* getting used to it." She raised tear-filled eyes to his.

Rand's next words surprised her speechless.

"Marry me, Krissy. Now. Not next year. Not even next month. Now, as soon as possible."

She stared at him, stunned. "But . . . but," she said, when she found her voice. "Rand, I've got these tests and possibly surgery ahead of me. I don't . . . we don't know what the future holds." She swallowed. "I . . . I don't even know if I have a future, if . . ."

"Stop that!" Rand ordered. "Krissy, bottom line is, no one knows if they have a future. I could step out into the street tomorrow and get run down by a truck, or have a sudden massive heart attack, or stroll down the sidewalk and be struck dead by a piece of a building falling on my head, or be fried by a bolt of lightning. Any one of us can."

She shook her head. "I know that. But that's just rationalizing on what *could* happen." She sighed. "But I *know* there's a lump in my breast. And with my family history it's very likely cancerous." She raised her hand to caress his taut cheek. "There's a big difference."

"Not to me." He turned his head and pressed his lips to her palm. "Krissy, I want you — need you — to be my wife, if it's for fifty years, or fifty days. Marry me, now. Please."

Oh, Lord, how could she refuse a proposal like that? Krissy asked herself, staring into his gentle eyes. "Rand, I don't know what to say."

Lowering his head, he brushed his lips over hers, murmuring, "Say yes, sweetheart."

A moment. A mere instant, really, then she sighed and brushed her lips over his.

"Yes."

CHAPTER 17

"Rand and I are getting married as soon as possible," Krissy announced to Jon and Julia as the four sat down in the restaurant. "Can you two come back to town sometime in the next few weeks? We really want you here with us."

Julia was shocked and delighted. "Wait a minute. I mean, of course we'll come, but when did you two decide to move up the wedding?"

Krissy flashed her famous smile, radiant and happy. "This afternoon. This man —" she slid a sparkling glance at Rand "— took advantage of my weakened state to coerce me into saying yes to his sudden brainstorm."

"I seem to recall it didn't take too much coercing," Rand defended himself.

Fascinated by the byplay between the couple, happy for her friend, and grateful to the man who had put the brightness back into Krissy's eyes, Julia shifted her gaze from one to the other, then to a smiling Jon.

"So, what do you guys think?" Rand directed his attention to them. "Do you approve?"

"Yes!" Julia and Jon spoke simultaneously.

"I think it's a wonderful idea," Julia continued. "Have you talked to Laura?"

Krissy shook her head. "Not yet. We fell asleep this afternoon and didn't wake up till it was time to get ready to meet you two. I'll call her tomorrow. You know I would love to have you and Laura for my matrons of honor."

"Well, I didn't actually know," Julia said, laughing softly. "But I do know I would have been crushed if you had asked anyone else to do it."

Krissy reached across the table to grab Julia's hand. "Oh, honey, you should have known. You and Laura weren't there the other times. I'm the one who'd be crushed if you weren't there this time —" she glanced at Rand "— with this man."

Though filled with happiness for Krissy, Julia felt a tiny pang at the loving look Rand was giving her friend. Without a word, he was telling her of his love for her. Jon used to look at her like that, Julia thought, with his heart and love in his eyes. He used to say the words, too, every day. Now . . . his voice echoed in her mind.

I missed you.

Where had his love gone? Julia asked herself, somehow maintaining her smile for her friend. It died, she thought. She had killed it.

She looked at Jon. He was watching her. She sighed with regret. He looked away.

Julia thought the evening would never end. But as she slid into bed, perilously close to tears, she determined once again to somehow corner Jon for a long, meaningful discussion.

Laura was as delighted as Julia had been by Krissy's news the next day. And, like Julia, she agreed immediately to being co-matron of honor. But she hadn't forgotten her friend's visit to the doctor.

"Krissy, honey, I'm very happy for you . . ." She paused, then hurried on, hopefully. "Does this mean your appointment with the doctor was encouraging?"

"Oh, Laura, not really," Krissy said, her voice shaded by a tinge of worry. "She is making arrangements for an ultrasound and biopsy. Then we'll see."

"So meanwhile you're going to get married?" Laura asked, infusing a bright note into her tone.

"Yes." The answer came back loud and clear.

By that morning, Krissy and Rand had settled on a date, time and place for the wedding.

"Next Saturday at ten, by a judge, in one of the private dining rooms in the hotel," she excitedly informed Laura.

"It sounds like the winning answer in a game of Clue!"

"It is a winning answer," Krissy replied. "But not in a game. This is the real thing. The very best thing."

"Are you calling me the very best?" Laura heard Rand's voice purr in the background.

"Yes, love, I am," Krissy said to him.

Laura suddenly felt envious of her dearest friend. "What should I wear? I mean for the wedding? Formal or what?"

"Oh, not formal," Krissy said. "Street clothes. A nice dress or suit . . . whatever."

Whatever. Moments later, Laura smiled as she hung up the receiver. How like Krissy. She'd very likely be decked out in a designer label dress valued at hundreds if not thousands of dollars. With shoes that cost even more.

There was nothing for it but to go shopping, Laura decided. Damn, she forgot to ask if she should bring the kids. They'd probably be bored. She'd ask her parents to watch them for a couple hours.

Oh, yeah, maybe Drew might want to go shopping for something new to wear to the wedding, too. Laura made a mental note to ask him when he got home . . . either tonight or when he got up for work tomorrow morning.

Surprisingly, Drew came home in time for dinner, though he did immediately tell Laura he had to go back to work later for a few hours.

Right, Laura thought, somehow maintaining her composure, while inside wanting to scream at him. To keep herself from losing it, and her self-respect with it, she launched into a recitation of Krissy's news.

"Again?" Drew shook his head, his tone sarcastic. "She's getting married again? How many does this make?"

"I hardly think that's relevant."

He shrugged. "Whatever."

Laura felt the spark of resentment inside her turn into anger. "She's asked Julie and me to be her co-matrons of honor," she said with a calm she was far from feeling. "I'm going shopping for a new dress and shoes. Is there anything I can get you? A shirt? Tie?"

"No." Drew's response was sharp and blunt. "I won't be needing anything new for the wedding, because I won't be attending the wedding."

"What? Why not?"

He shot her an impatient look. "I have plans for a golf game on Saturday."

The anger in Laura burned hotter. "Instead of going with me to one of my best friends' wedding, you're going to play golf?"

"You heard me." A shadow passed over his impatient expression. "I'm not changing my plans just to traipse into town and watch your bimbo friend marry yet another sucker." He sneered. "Tell me, is Rand as rich as the others were?"

Her anger flared out of control and something strange came over Laura. Where she had never fought for herself, she became a fierce defender of her friend. "I don't know, or care, if Rand is rich. It's none of my . . . or your business. And, in all honesty, I don't care if you go or not. In fact, I'd rather go without you."

"Why?" He cast a demeaning glance over the length of her. "Have the urge to try something, or someone, different?"

"You . . . you . . ." By now, Laura was

so mad she could barely speak.

"What?" he challenged her.

"You son of a bitch." She wasn't merely calling names, she thought. She always *had* thought his mother was a bitch. "You . . . you dare suggest that I . . ." She shuddered with rage. "Damn you!" she shouted. "Golf my ass. I know where you're going, and who you'll be with." She gave a dismissive wave of her hand. "Why wait till after dinner? Go to your girlfriend now."

Drew stared at her in amazement for a moment, as though he couldn't believe she had actually said what she had. Then, grabbing his suit coat from the back of the chair where he'd draped it, he strode to the door. "Okay, I will," he said belligerently. "And you can go to hell."

"And for all I care," she shouted after him, incensed, "don't come back at all."

"Good," he shouted back at her. "Suits me. I'll send for my things."

The door slammed shut. Trembling in reaction, Laura stared at it, relief washing through her. Relief not only because she had finally found the guts to let him know how she felt, but relief that the kids weren't home to hear it all.

She thought.

"Mom?"

Oh, dear God. When did Drew Jr. come in? She whirled around to see him standing in the archway, all six feet, three inches of him. His face was somber, his eyes shadowed.

"Oh, honey, I'm so . . ." Laura bit her lip.

He shook his head. "No, Mom, it's all right." Crossing to her, he gave her a hug. "I knew he was fooling around."

For the first time in a long time, Laura felt comforted, safe within the embrace of her tall, strong and very bright son. "How long have you known?" she mumbled into the green eagle emblazoned on his soft cotton T-shirt.

"I figured it out a couple of years ago," he said, dropping his arms and stepping back. "I . . ." He gulped a deep, shuddering breath. "I want to punch his face in for cheating on you. How could he? You're the best wife and mother in the world."

"Ah, honey, thank you." Laura sniffed. "And you're not too bad as a son, either," she said, managing a weak smile. "How am I going to tell your brother and sisters? They love him, and they're going to be hurt."

"And you're not?"

"Yes, I am." She sighed. "And yet, I'm

254

not as hurt as I thought I'd be. It may sound terrible, Drew, but I feel strangely light. Free."

He shook his head. "Nothing terrible or strange about it, Mom. I know you've put up with his cheating for years. And you did it for us kids." His smile was tender and suddenly mature. "I'll help you tell the others, make them understand."

How had they managed to raise such a wonderful son? No, not "they." Drew had hardly ever been home. *She* had somehow managed to raise this terrific kid, who was now a man.

Laura felt tears of pride sting her eyes for her tall, handsome son. What had she done to be so blessed?

Saturday dawned bright and hot. The phone rang as Julia was dressing to go to Philadelphia, and fretting because Jon wasn't home from his Saturday-morning appointments.

Why couldn't he have rescheduled, she thought, fuming as she lifted the receiver.

"Julia!" Krissy cried before Julia could even say hello. "I'm a nervous wreck. I feel sick . . . or like I want to run away and hide."

"What's the matter? Did you change your mind?" she asked.

"No, no, I do want to get married," Krissy said, a little wildly. "But, well, I'm used merchandise. I'm ten years older and not nearly good enough for him."

Jon strolled into the bedroom, arching his eyebrows at the concerned expression on Julia's face.

Krissy, bridal nerves, she mouthed.

He rolled his eyes and yanked at his tie, whispering, "Have fun, I'm going to grab a shower."

Julia made a face at him, then said soothingly into the phone, "Krissy, that is simply not true."

"I *am* ten years older than him!"

"I didn't mean about the age difference," Julia said. "I meant about you not being good enough for him. And too used? Tell me he hasn't had his share of lovers?"

"But he didn't marry them." She sniffled.

Julia sighed around a smile. "Okay, so you did. So what? Do you love him?"

"Oh, Julie, so much it scares the hell out of me," she wailed.

"And I believe Rand truly loves you."

"So do I," Krissy admitted meekly.

Julia's eyes flew wide. Krissy meek was

256

damned startling. "So, what's the problem then?"

"I don't know." There was a slight pause before she heaved a sigh. "I'm being silly, aren't I?"

"Yes, because you are nervous. But I do believe that's normal behavior for all brides on their wedding day."

"I never was before. I wonder why?" Krissy mused. "Isn't that strange?"

"No." Julia smiled. "You weren't marrying Rand before. Did you love the others as much?"

Krissy was quiet for a moment. "You know, I thought I was in love before. But the way I felt then didn't come close to this scared feeling."

"And I'll bet he feels the same way."

"Oh, hon, I wish, but I seriously doubt it."

"Where is he now?"

"In the shower."

"When he comes out, ask him how he feels."

"I can't do that!"

"I double dare you," Julia challenged, as if they were grade-schoolers again.

"Well . . ." Krissy drew a deep, audible breath. "Maybe."

"Goodbye, Krissy," Julia said, grinning.

"I'll see you in a few hours."

"Bye, hon, thanks for listening to me whine."

"Anytime, dear heart."

"Anytime, what?" Jon asked, coming out of their bathroom as she hung up the phone.

"She had the jitters," she explained, aching inside as she watched him step into boxer shorts. After twenty years, he was still lean and muscular . . . with an attractive, tight butt. "She thanked me for calming her down."

"Well, she has a lot of stress right now," he said, sitting on the side of the bed to pull on his socks. "It's only normal if she's jittery."

Julia just stared at him in disbelief for a moment. How could he understand Krissy's emotional state so well now, when he hadn't understood her own feelings, her stress and fear about anyone other than him performing surgery on Emily?

"Are you ready?" Busy stepping into his suit pants, Jon hadn't turned to look at her.

Julia was acutely tempted to broadside him with a complete list of her emotional state then and there, but quickly brought herself up short, before she could open her mouth and let fly. It may have been the place, but it certainly was not the time. With the work schedule he had been keeping, there never seemed to be enough time for a long, meaningful discussion.

And Julia was getting pretty damn tired of living on the edge of what appeared to be an ever widening chasm between them.

"Julia?" Jon finally turned to look, frown at her. "Is something wrong?"

"No . . . er, I was worrying about Krissy," she said, which wasn't a complete lie, Julia assured herself. She really was worried about her friend.

"Well, worrying isn't going to change anything."

No kidding, Sherlock, Julia thought, irritated with the complacency most males appeared to possess. Problem was, they never offered an answer for how to turn off the worry.

"You know," he continued, supremely unaware of the annoyance biting at her. "This lump in Krissy's breast might not be as bad as she has herself believing it is."

"I know," Julia was forced to agree. She also felt compelled to remind him of a very salient point. "But, considering she watched her mother die of breast cancer, I think she has cause to be *stressed.*"

"Yes, of course," he agreed, rather quickly, as if aware he was on the losing side of this discussion. In the process of buttoning his shirt, he raised his eyebrows at her, and changed the subject. "Are you just about ready?"

"I have my makeup to do, that's all." She started for the bathroom.

"The girls?"

She didn't stop moving, or glance aside to look at him. "Your sister picked them up an hour ago. They were going shopping, then to a movie."

"My sister spoils them." Humor laced his voice.

"I know." Julia stepped into the bathroom, but left the door open.

"She should have had some of her own kids to spoil." The touch of humor was replaced by a sad note. His sister and brother-in-law had never been able to have a baby. So they doted on his and Julia's daughters.

"I know," Julia repeated in soft compassion. Putting the finishing touches to her makeup, she walked into the bedroom. Catching Jon's eye in the mirror as he adjusted his necktie, she announced, "I'm ready. Will I do?"

He ran a long glance over her body from head to toe, his expression changing to one of surprise. "You look . . . fantastic." A slow, almost sensuous smile of admiration curved his lips. "Is that a new dress?"

Julia was struck speechless for a second. *The dress.* The one she had bought early in the spring in hope of getting his full attention. Well, it was now months later, but it had certainly elicited the response she had hoped for. Warmth spread through her. It had been so long since he had complimented her on her appearance, never mind looked at her the way he was now.

He swung open the bedroom door. The motion restarted her mental and speech process. "Thank you. Yes, the dress is new. It's one of the things I bought on my mad shopping spree last spring . . . when I spent so much money."

"And worth whatever you paid for it."

She swept a glance the length of his body. "You look quite handsome yourself." She met his avid perusal. "Not many men look that good in a tux."

"Yeah, yeah," he grinned, following her from the room and shutting the door behind him. "I'm a regular movie star." His grin broadened. "Like Rand."

"Sorry." Suddenly feeling light, easy, she grinned back at him. "I can't think of any man as handsome as Rand."

CHAPTER 18

When she and Jon checked into the hotel, Julia was surprised when they were shown to a suite, compliments of Krissy and Rand.

"This friend of yours knows how to live," Jon said, taking stock of the two rooms.

"This friend of mine," Julia echoed, "is loaded, and I'm sure Rand isn't on his economic knees, either."

Jon opened his mouth to respond, as a trill of the phone sounded. "Krissy," he said, smiling. "Wanna bet?"

"No." Julia shook her head, smiling back as she reached for the receiver. "Hello?"

"Julia! I knew you were in, I called the desk." Krissy now sounded the exact opposite of jittery; she sounded bubbly. Julia wondered if she had been into the wedding champagne. "Honey," she bubbled on, "I need you up here, Laura's already on her way. Can Rand and Drew come to your suite?"

Julia frowned. "Yes, of course. Is something wrong?"

"Wrong?" She laughed. "No, everything is perfect, unbelievably perfect. You'll be delighted to know how perfect. It's just that —" she hesitated, then laughed again "— I threw Rand out of the suite, told him he couldn't see my dress. He was so cranky. 'What am I supposed to do, hang out in the lobby in my tux?' he asked me. Isn't he adorable?" She didn't wait for an answer. "Will you come?"

"I'll be up in a few minutes. Okay?"

"Okay."

"Will you unpack for us, Jon?" she asked, replacing the receiver on the base. "Krissy wants Laura and me to come up to help her dress."

"What about Rand?" A knock on the door came on the heels of his question.

"I believe that's him now," she said, unable to suppress a giggle. "Seems like Krissy's acting like a first-time bride. She won't let him see her dress."

Jon rolled his eyes and went to the door.

Rand strolled in, grinning. "Isn't this fun, kids?"

Julia made for the door. "I'm outta here." She pulled the door open and cried "Oh!" at finding a young man standing there, hand raised to rap on the door.

"Drew?" Julia asked, recognizing Laura's son from the pictures she'd shown them.

"Yeah." He nodded with a boyish grin. "I'm Mom's escort for the wedding."

"Oh," she said again, wondering where Drew Sr. was as she stepped aside to allow him to enter.

After Drew Jr. was inside, Julia made the introductions, gave Jon a telling look, silently asking him to take care of the young man, and left.

She had a few questions for Laura.

Julia didn't get a chance to ask her questions for some time. Everything else flew out of her mind at the announcement Krissy made the minute Julia entered the suite.

"I'm clean," Krissy blurted out, laughing as tears ran down her face. "I got a call from the doctor half an hour ago. The radiologist thought it was a cyst when he read the ultrasound, but the doctor wanted a biopsy to be certain. I had the biopsy the day after the ultrasound. That's why my doctor called today — my wedding day — to tell me it's a benign cyst. She said we'll leave it go for now, but she wants to check it every six months, to see if it's getting larger."

Julia and Laura ran to hug her at the same time.

Arms around one another, they laughed and cried together for quite a while. When they finally parted, they all three got a case of the giggles at the sight of one another's mascara-smeared eyes.

"Ahhh, ladies, we've got work to do," said Julia, always the practical one, glad she had had the foresight to bring her makeup bag with her.

It was while they were repairing the damage to their faces that Julia remembered to ask "Where's Drew, Laura?"

Krissy frowned, glancing from Laura to Julia. "Isn't he in your suite with Jon and Rand?"

"No, Drew Jr. came with me."

Both Julia and Krissy gazed at Laura, waiting for her to explain.

Laura drew a deep breath. "Drew Sr. is on the golf course as we speak . . . I think. From there I suspect he will be staying with his latest girlfriend." She sneered.

"What?" Krissy yelped.

"Are you serious?" Julia asked.

"Yes." Laura drew another breath. "I tossed the cheating bastard out." She shrugged. "Well, I didn't physically toss him out. I had finally had enough," she explained. "You see, I found out by accident that Drew was having an affair with a woman named Megan . . . our real estate agent, of all people."

"Did you confront the creep?" Krissy said, visibly outraged for Laura.

"No. I've been trying to decide what to do for weeks. There was, is, so much to consider. The kids. The house." She sighed. "I didn't know what to do. Then Drew decided for me when I told him about the wedding." She paused and neither friend felt inclined to interrupt her recitation.

"He said he wouldn't be attending because he had made plans for an afternoon golf game and dinner afterward." She shook her head. "The very same excuse he used last week for leaving, when I wanted to wait here until you got back from seeing the doctor. I swear the man believes I'm either that stupid or unconscious."

"You are neither one of those," Julia said.

"Yeah!" Krissy agreed.

"I know, but thanks, guys." She smiled, if wanly. "Anyway, I got so angry, I told him to go to his game, and his girlfriend, and don't bother to come back."

"And what did he say?" Krissy said.

"He said, 'fine, I'll send for my things' and slammed out the door."

"Oh, honey, I'm so sorry," Julia said, taking Laura into her arms to offer a comforting hug.

Laura hugged her back and shook her head. "Don't be. I'm not. Made me get my thoughts together. Oh, for a few minutes, I didn't know what to think, what to do. I didn't know Drew Jr. had overheard everything until he came to me, saying everything would be okay. He told me he had figured out some time ago his father was seeing other women. He's behind me one hundred percent, even helped me tell the other kids."

"Good for him," Krissy said.

"He's a good-looking boy," Julia put in.

Laura beamed. "Yes, isn't he? And, more importantly," she added, "Drew Jr. has his head on straight."

"So now what?" Krissy asked.

"Now I get a lawyer and a divorce." She paused. "My kids will always come first with me, but I think it's time for me to be my own person. I even thought about taking some college courses, finally get my degree."

"About time you thought of yourself for once," Julia said.

"Go for it!" Krissy chimed in. "When do you begin?"

"Now." Laura laughed. "I can't tell you how . . . relieved and free I feel. And I've promised myself I'd keep the Laura ball rolling."

"That's just so . . ." Krissy began, when the ringing of the phone interrupted. "Oh, damn," she said, turning to the phone. "Who could that be, today of all . . ." She happened to glance at her watch. "Oh, my God! Look at the time. I'll bet that's Rand, wondering if I'm going to stand him up!"

There were a few minutes of frantic activity as the three women made last-minute finishing touches to faces, hair and clothes. Then, laughing like schoolgirls, they dashed from the suite to the elevator.

"You know what?" Krissy said as the elevator descended. "I've promised myself that this time, I'd make this marriage work. Ten-year age difference be damned."

The wedding was brief, but lovely. Krissy looked as close to angelic as was possible for Krissy. She wore an off-white, street-length sheath that somehow appeared demure while hugging her fantastic curves.

The movie director stood as Rand's best man, while Julia and Laura stood to the right of the beautiful and glowing bride. Rand gazed at his bride with love and devotion in his eyes during the entire short ceremony.

The reception was held in the same small conference room, lavishly decorated in white and gold. The cake rose three tiers, with white rosebuds and tiny golden leaves. A bride and groom embraced on the top tier. The bride had red hair the exact same shade as Krissy's.

The dinner served after the ceremony was perfectly prepared, and absolutely delicious. The champagne was French and, Julia knew, outrageously expensive.

Julia and Jon both indulged in two glasses each. She danced with Rand and Drew Jr. Jon danced with Krissy and Laura. They danced together twice.

Hours later, as they entered their suite, Julia was humming the music from the last dance they had shared.

"Have a good time?" Jon asked, smiling at her as he loosened his bow tie.

"Hmmm," Julia murmured, musing there was something very sexy about the ends of a black bow tie lying against a man's white dress shirt.

"Sleepy?"

Uh-oh, Julia thought, an unexpected tingle of excitement tightening inside. "Errr, not very."

"Good." Slowly starting to walk to her, he began to unbutton his shirt.

Julia felt her pulse leap. Then she brought herself up short. No. Not this time. She would not fall into bed with him without talking first.

Julia held up her hand to place it against his chest. "We need to talk, Jon."

"Now?"

"Now," she said with flat determination.

"Jul . . . ie," he said softly.

Jul . . . ie, my foot, she thought. He only ever used that coaxing tone when he wanted something, and she hadn't heard it in several years.

"I mean it, Jon." She stood firm, staring him down.

He sighed, but folded. "Okay. Would you like more wine while we talk? There's a supply in the credenza."

Julia shook her head. "No, no more wine. But can you call room service for a pot of decaf coffee, a large pot, while I change?"

"Okay." He moved to the phone. "But I hate for you to change out of that dress."

Pleased by his remark, Julia went into

the bathroom to change, clean her face and brush her teeth. When she returned to the sitting room in her nightgown and robe, Jon was sprawled in a chair, watching the early news.

"Coffee not here yet?" Dumb question, she chided herself, since it was nowhere in sight.

"No." He stood up stretching. "I may as well change before it gets here." He handed her a bill. "That should be enough to cover the coffee and the tip."

The coffee arrived a few minutes before Jon walked back into the room, dressed in pajama pants and a silk robe. Julia had already poured cups for both of them. He picked up the cup, cradling it as he sat opposite her.

"Okay, Julia, what's this all about?"

"Us." She gently blew on the hot beverage before trying a sip.

"What about us?" His voice held a wary note.

Julia took another, bolstering sip. "About whether or not we're going to stay together."

Jon nearly choked. "Are you telling me you want a divorce?"

"Is that what you want?" Julia asked, sounding steady, feeling quivery inside.

271

"Me? No!" He stared at her in amazement. "I didn't start this." He stopped, closed his eyes as he grimaced, then opening his eyes again said, "Or maybe I did."

Thrown off by his statement, Julia stared at him. "What do you mean, maybe you did?"

"Julia, I should have told you this from the beginning." He stopped to take a deep — strength gathering? — breath.

Oh, God, no. Brooke. She felt sick and had to force the question through her dry throat. "Tell me what?"

Though Jon hesitated a moment longer, he met her intent gaze squarely. "I performed the surgery on Emily."

She blinked, thrown even further off-kilter. In the next instant, the full content of his confession hit her. "You did what? What are you saying?"

"I'm saying I performed most of the surgery on Emily," he repeated, going on to explain. "Halfway through the procedure, Doctor Michaelson felt light-headed, almost fell. One of the assistants caught him. It quickly passed, but he no longer felt safe doing the surgery. Emily was prepped, out cold on the table. He told me I'd have to do it . . . and I did." He grabbed another quick breath. "I'm sorry I didn't tell you before."

"Jon . . . I . . ." Julia shook her head, angry and mystified. "After the way I had begged you to do it yourself —" She paused in an attempt to control herself. It didn't help. Jumping up, she shouted at him, "Damn you, why the hell didn't you tell me then, or at any time since?"

"Julia," he said with careful patience. "Please calm . . ."

"No!" she yelled over his even tones. "I won't calm down. You have been keeping this from me for years. I want an answer. Now!"

"Okay." He tried a smile; it was more a grimace. "Maybe it was pride or maybe stupidity . . ." Again her scathing voice cut across his, shocking him.

"No shit, Dick Tracy."

Jon stared at her in sheer amazement.

Julia understood why. She never used that kind of language. She thought it at times, but never used it.

"I'm waiting." She prompted him.

"I was hurt," he suddenly blurted. "Dammit, Julia, you worked in the medical field, around doctors for years. You should have known, understood why I was so unwilling to perform the surgery." He shuddered. "For God's sake, Julia. She's my, our baby. One tiny tremor in my hand and . . . I could have killed her, and if I had, I would have killed myself." Tears pooled in his eyes. "Jesus Christ, Julia, what's hard to understand about that?"

Julia was stunned by his outcry. His words were more prayer than curse. Tears ran down his face.

She had never seen Jon cry before, not even when their babies were born. She had always believed he was simply the type of man who thought it unmanly to weep. Maybe she had been wrong all along.

Maybe she had been wrong about a lot of things.

Any maybe it was time for confessions all around.

"I'm sorry." Julia lowered her eyes, ashamed to meet his gaze. "I knew all along that I was wrong to insist you do the surgery." She raised her eyes, bit her lips, sighed. "You see, I did understand . . . but I was so terrified. And I believed absolutely that you were the very best for Emily." Tears stung her own eyes. "I understood, and still I've been harboring resentment all this time, letting it color my feelings, my life."

"Thank you."

The soft sound of his voice, his words, startled her.

"For what? For resenting you all this time?"

He smiled, sadly. "No, Julia, for having the courage to tell me after all this time."

"Have you been working up to telling me you want a divorce?" Jon asked.

"I've thought about it," she answered with blunt honesty. "Neither one of us can claim the last years have been . . ." She broke off, shrugging.

"No, neither one of us can," he agreed, mirroring her shrug.

"It's certainly been no bed of roses."

"It's hardly been any bed at all," he came back at her, making an obvious point.

"What about Brooke?" she retorted.

"What about her?"

"Have you slept with her?" Her anger was showing again. She didn't care, it was better than revealing the pain of feeling betrayed.

"No. No. No." Jon exploded. *"I told you I had not been intimate with her."*

"You don't call kissing her intimate?" she cried. "Not just once, but several times?"

"Okay." He was breathing heavily, but he had managed to calm his voice. "Yes, as I told you, I kissed her, several times but that was all. I couldn't do it, Julia, but I admit I was tempted, very tempted. What man whose wife was distant wouldn't be?"

Julia stiffened. "I never refused you, turned you away, had a *headache*."

"I know that, Julia." He rubbed a hand over his face, suddenly looking tired. "But you were so passive, showed very little feeling." A half smile flickered over his lips. "Until the last couple of times." He flicked a hand to indicate their surroundings. "That night in this hotel. You were on fire."

"I was experiencing the same thing you were feeling," she said in the most dignified tone she could muster. "Lust. Old-fashioned, down and dirty, lust."

"Works for me." He had the audacity to grin at her.

Julia pulled a stern face to keep from grinning back at him. "I hear it does for most men."

Jon swept a slow, suggestive look over her. "For many women, too."

Her spark of humor died. "If lust is all that's left between us, there's not much hope for our marriage, is there?"

"Do you expect the carefree days of our youth to last forever?" he said, beginning to look beaten and strangely hopeless.

"I'm not a silly fool, Jon. I know the excitement of first love can't possibly last. I've always known that." She heard his soft sigh of relief, but she wasn't finished.

"I've also always known that a marriage doesn't have to deteriorate into long silences and loneliness either. There's always the hope of laughter, companionship, as a couple grow old together."

"You're saying I'm away from home too much."

Julia wasn't about to pull her punches. "Yes, you are not home enough, and I think it's deliberate."

Jon bristled. "I do have a large practice, you know."

Julia sighed, beginning to feel defeated. "I know you do. I also know you no longer need to put in those long hours. You've been hiding, taking any and all patients to keep from coming home."

He looked down, as if fascinated by his shoes. "Maybe I didn't think there was any reason to come home." He glanced up, challenge in his expression. "Is there?"

The air of defeat dissipated. "Yes, there's our daughters, who love you very much." She drew a quick breath. "And there's me. I still live there, you know. And I still love you."

"I'm glad, about both. Because I still love you. I always will." He swallowed, smiled. "I'll start trimming my patient list Monday. It may take a while."

She smiled back. "That's okay. I won't be lonely after the girls go back to school. You see, I'm going back to work."

"What?" Jon frowned. "Why?"

Julia shrugged. "Because I want to."

"Oh." The frown disappeared. "Where?"

Julia laughed, the easiest she had laughed while with him in much too long a time. "I'm going back to radiology. I've already talked to Jim Murro, the new head of the department?" He nodded. "He suggested I start by following around a tech to bring me up to speed. I start the day after the girls go back to school."

"What about all your other activities?"

This time she allowed herself a wide grin. "I was planning to start trimming back Monday."

Jon began to laugh, the same joyful laugh he'd had before Emily's fall.

Laughing with him, Julia slid her hand into his and led him to the bedroom.

A little healthy lust never hurt an aging marriage . . . or the couple in it.

ABOUT THE AUTHOR

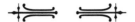

In 2004, **Joan Hohl** celebrated twenty-five years of being a published writer. She has written over fifty books — she claims she doesn't know the exact number as she gave up counting somewhere between thirty-five and forty! She has been on the *New York Times*, *USA Today* and Waldenbooks lists, and has won several awards, including the Romance Writers of America RITA® Award, two *Romantic Times* Reviewer's Choice awards and is on *Romantic Times'* 100 Best Romances List. She has published works in several genres, including romance, single-title women's fiction, historical and time travel.

Joan lives in Pennsylvania with Marv, her husband of fifty-two years. They have two daughters, Lori and Amy, two grandchildren, Erica and Cammeron, and one great-grandchild.

We hope you have enjoyed this Large Print book. Other Thorndike, Wheeler or Chivers Press Large Print books are available at your library or directly from the publishers.

For more information about current and upcoming titles, please call or write, without obligation, to:

Publisher
Thorndike Press
295 Kennedy Memorial Drive
Waterville, ME   04901
Tel. (800) 223-1244

Or visit our Web site at:
www.gale.com/thorndike
www.gale.com/wheeler

OR

Chivers Large Print
published by BBC Audiobooks Ltd
St James House, The Square
Lower Bristol Road
Bath BA2 3BH
England
Tel. +44(0) 800 136919
email: bbcaudiobooks@bbc.co.uk
www.bbcaudiobooks.co.uk

All our Large Print titles are designed for easy reading, and all our books are made to last.